Lawrence is one of the council assassins, perhaps the one who ended up with the worst ability—he's a snake shifter, and he secretes his venom even in his human form. He's never been able to eliminate it entirely from his saliva and bloodstream, and that means he's made sure to stay away from sex and hookups as much as possible—until now. When he's sent to kidnap the son of Gavin White, the man experimenting on shifters, he discovers Griffith is his mate.

Griffith is a geneticist. He works for a shifter-owned company that tries to help the shifters and humans who were experimented on by the Glass Research Company. When he's kidnapped by a cute blond who tells him his father is doing the opposite—experimenting on shifters to turn them into war machines—he's horrified, and he wants to help.

Lawrence has no idea what to do with the knowledge that Griffith is his mate. They can't bond, not with the venom in Lawrence's saliva, so he decides not to tell Griffith about it. He hasn't counted on Griffith's stubbornness, though, and when he has to rush to help his mate, he knows he won't be able to stay away, even though it would be the right thing to do.

Lawrence
Copyright © 2019 Catherine Lievens
ISBN: 978-1-4874-2608-8
Cover art by Angela Waters

Published by eXtasy Books Inc or
Devine Destinies, an imprint of eXtasy Books Inc

Look for us online at:
www.eXtasybooks.com or www.devinedestinies.com

LAWRENCE
COUNCIL ASSASSINS BOOK 7

BY

CATHERINE LIEVENS

CHAPTER ONE

Lawrence threw popcorn at North's head. When North whipped his head around to find out who the culprit was, Lawrence kept his focus on the TV. He knew he wouldn't fool North — he had a bucket of popcorn in his lap after all — but it was fun to watch North hesitate about accusing him. He looked from Lawrence to Ulric, who was stuffing his face with the popcorn and would probably have to be paid to waste food by throwing it around.

"Not funny, guys," North grumbled.

Lawrence disagreed, but when he reached into the bucket again, he hit Ulric's hand. He wrinkled his nose. "Dude. Are you trying to seduce me or something? We're not in a theater."

"And you're not my type," Ulric said without looking away from the TV. Lawrence wasn't sure why Ulric was so focused on the superhero movie. He'd already seen it about a dozen times. The actors were hot, but didn't it get boring after the fifth or sixth time?

"I'm everyone's type," Lawrence said.

Ulric finally looked at him. "Yeah? How come you don't date, then?"

Shit. Ulric knew better than to bring that up. Lawrence could see he already regretted it from his expression, so he forced himself to smile. "Because no one is good enough for me."

"Law —"

"It's fine. Promise."

Ulric sighed. "I shouldn't have said that."

"In his defense, he was focused on the Captain's ass," North said.

Lawrence relaxed. "Who wouldn't be? I mean, I don't care about superheroes, but the way they look makes it worth having to watch this *again*."

Ulric groaned. "That's all you got from the movie?"

Lawrence loved to tease him about the things he liked—namely, superheroes and food. "Was there anything else to get?"

And just like that, everything was right again. Lawrence settled deeper into the couch and listened to his best friend explain what he'd missed from the movie—and apparently, there was a lot. Lawrence didn't care much. The main reason he was watching the movie right now was that he liked spending time with his friends. It had become harder since North had bonded, even though both he and his mate still lived at the warehouse. North spent more time with Milo now, as was right, but Lawrence missed him. He still had Ulric—when his face wasn't in a bucket of popcorn—and Miles, but it wasn't the same.

Things were changing. A lot of the assassins had found their mates, and it left Lawrence nervous. It was almost like an epidemic, except there was no vaccine against it.

Lawrence would have grabbed two of them if they existed.

It wasn't that he didn't want to meet his mate. He'd love to have what North had with Milo, what Win had with Graham, what all the other couples had. He wished he *could* have it. But even if he did meet his mate, there was no way the two of them could ever be more than platonic friends, and that wouldn't be right. Lawrence didn't want to condemn his mate to a life of being nothing more than friends, not when they should have more.

The door to the stairs clicked open, and Win came in. He

was holding a bunch of files, and that could only mean one thing — meeting time.

Ulric groaned and waved his greasy hand toward the TV. "Can't we finish watching this before you explain how fucked up the world is?" he asked.

He'd known better, of course, and Lawrence doubted he was surprised by the look Win gave him. "You can continue watching until everyone else is here, but once they are, you'll turn it off, or at the very least, pause it. We have work to do."

Ulric continued to grumble under his breath. Lawrence didn't blame him. He loved his job, even though he hated the reason he was there to do it in the first place, but the past several months had been fucked up. The job hadn't been that different, but instead of going after serial killers and rapists, they'd gone after people out to get them.

Lawrence didn't understand how people could still be so hateful when shifters had been out for fifteen years, although he supposed that watching humans deal with people who were a different color or who loved someone of the same sex should have been a big clue. Win hadn't officially told anyone yet, but Lawrence had heard that shifters were as involved in this mess as humans were, and he wasn't surprised about that either. Some people didn't care who they had to cut down to become rich.

It took some time to gather everyone who wasn't out on a job. It always did. Win was patient, although the fact that he was softly talking with Roark and Beck might have something to do with it. He probably didn't even notice how much time had passed.

He looked up and blinked, then did a quick head count before clearing his throat. "All right. People, you can take a copy of this," he said, handing out the stack to Cora, who was sitting closest to him. "You'll have time to go over it later. It contains everything we know about the Beasts."

Lawrence frowned. "The Beasts?"

"Yes. They allied themselves with the group of people who were trying to kill us, and with the government."

There was a moment of absolute silence as everyone digested that. The government was supposed to be on their side. They were supposed to protect shifters the way shifters protected humans. The council worked with the government to make sure hate crimes and whatnot were taken care of.

And now they were working *against* shifters?

"You all know I met with Evan's father."

"Can we *not* call him that, please?" Evan asked.

"Of course. I apologize. I met with Moore, the last man who remained of the group of people who tried to kill us. I got some answers from him."

"And that answer was that he was sent by the government?" Ulric asked.

"Not exactly. He's human, as you might know, and he's been selling shifters to the government. To do that, he's been in contact with the Beasts, who pick up shifters and hand them over to him, who then sells them. That's the main reason he was in this. He wanted the council gone so he could continue with this."

"So we have two enemies to face," North mused.

"Yes, although the council wants us to focus on the government. We're almost a hundred percent sure that we're only dealing with a small part of it, a hidden part of it. We're going to have to find out who's involved apart from Gavin White, which is the name Moore gave me."

"What about the Beasts?"

"The enforcers will take the lead on that. I'm not saying we won't help, but the Beasts are shifters, and they operate under the light of the sun. On the other hand, the part of the government behind this is hidden, like us."

"So do we get to kill this White guy?" Ulric asked.

"Not yet. That's probably going to be our endgame, but the council wants answers first, and I think we can all agree that we need them. Gavin White is only one man. There's no way he's the only one involved in this, and we *have* to find out who else is."

"Do you have an idea of what the government is doing with the shifters they're buying?" Lawrence asked, even though he had a pretty good idea. The people around him, and he, himself, were proof of what humans were ready to do to shifters.

Win sighed. "They're experimenting on them, just like Glass did. I have no idea yet of what kind of experiments or any details, but that's what we're going to have to work on. We need names, numbers, documents, anything we can get our hands on."

"Who's going to take care of White?" Because someone had to, even if it was only to follow him around.

Win leaned back in his chair. He looked at Roark and Beck, then cleared his throat. "We have an idea about that. I'm sure not everyone is going to be happy about it, but the council agrees that this is what we need right now."

Lawrence leaned forward. "Well? What are you talking about?"

"We're going to kidnap White's son, and we're sending you, Lawrence."

Griffith rubbed his eyes. They burned, a sure sign he'd spent too much time in front of his computer. But then he always spent too much time in front of his computer. If he wasn't in the lab, he was at his desk.

But not tonight. Tonight, he had plans. They might not be what most people would think of as fun plans, but he was looking forward to it.

His phone rang just as he got to his car. He managed to wrestle it out of his pocket before it stopped ringing, but he wished he hadn't when he saw the caller was his mother. He could probably ignore it, but she'd call again, so he might as well get through this now that he wasn't working. "Mom," he said as he answered.

"Honey. I hope I'm not bothering you."

"No." Griffith unlocked his car and opened the driver door.

"Are you sure? You're not still at work, are you? You work too much, and it's already past seven."

"I just left." He threw his messenger bag into the passenger seat and sat behind the wheel.

"That's good. Are you coming over for dinner?"

Griffith would rather get a root canal than have dinner with his father. "No, sorry. I already have plans."

"Is it a date?" His mother's voice was hesitant. She was no doubt torn between wanting him to have someone in his life and be happy and her husband's belief that Griffith being gay was wrong and against God's law — whatever that meant.

"No. I'm going to the shelter." That was probably worse than being gay in his father's eyes. At least Griffith could try to ignore the gay part of himself, be celibate and lead a good, God-fearing life, but no. Instead, he lived to disgrace his father's good name by not only being gay but also volunteering with a teen LGBTQ shelter.

The horror.

"You know your father doesn't like you working there," Griffith's mother said.

That was part of the reason Griffith did it, but he wasn't about to admit that. "I know, and I don't care. Me being gay isn't going to change, whatever he thinks or says, and those kids need all the help they can get. And I *volunteer* there, Mom. It's not a job."

"Maybe you could do that at an animal shelter?"

And there they went again. "Nope, but don't worry about it. You don't have to tell Dad why I'm not coming over." He probably didn't care about not seeing Griffith, but he *would* freak out if Griffith's mom told him *why* he wasn't there. His mom knew that, so she'd probably keep her mouth shut.

She sighed. "I don't see you often enough."

Griffith agreed with that. If only she'd stop catering to his asshole father and divorce him, Griffith would see her every week. But there was no way he wanted to spend the time it would take to have dinner with his father, not unless he *had* to. "I'm sorry, Mom, but you know that until Dad gets over his hang-ups, I'm sticking to Thanksgiving and Christmas." If even that.

"He feels strongly about everything, Griffith, and you can't deny he might not be wrong."

"About what? Me being an abomination? Or shifters being born of the devil?" Those were two things his father mentioned every time he saw Griffith. He was nothing if not an asshole.

"Griffith—"

"No, Mom." Griffith wasn't sure how he'd managed to come out of his teenage years sane of mind and not a ball of hate like his father was. "I'm sorry, but I can't share his views of the world."

"But you're not a shifter."

"Maybe not, but I *am* gay. And even if I weren't, I doubt I'd think that shifters are animals like he does. They're not. We're never going to see eye to eye about this, and that's okay." Griffith had given up trying to convince his father otherwise. He just avoided him now.

"But you could find another job."

That was a hard no. Griffith *loved* what he did, no matter how much his father disapproved. He wanted to help people, and not just humans. That was why he was working on un-doing the genetic damage that had been done to some of them. It was very slow work, but at least he felt he was help-ing, not like his father, who did who-knew-what for the gov-ernment. Griffith was lucky he'd been hired by a private wealthy shifter whose daughter had been captured by the Glass Research Company back in the day. She hadn't made it out alive, and the man had sworn to do what he could to undo the damage the company had created.

Griffith was proud to be part of that, just like he was proud of the work he did as a volunteer with the shelter.

"I have to go, Mom," Griffith said. He already knew no one would change their mind, so it was no use insisting. Maybe he could take his mother out for lunch next week to catch up with her. He'd never been sure if she believed what his father spouted or if she just went along to keep the peace in their home, and he wasn't sure he cared at this point. Still, she was his mother, and he loved her.

"All right. Call me when you get home."

"I'll text you, and you don't need to worry. I told you there are only teenagers at the shelter. They're not going to hurt me."

"You can't be sure of that."

Griffith wasn't going to win this, so he let it go. "I'll text you," he repeated.

He was glad when he could finally hang up. He loved his mother, but he hated his father, and he hated how subservient his mother was to him even more. It was like she'd be entirely lost if she wasn't married to him, and in part, Griffith could understand that, considering how long they'd been together. That didn't mean he had to like it, though—and he didn't.

But that wasn't a problem for now. It wasn't going any-where, because his *mother* wasn't going anywhere, unfortu-nately.

Griffith drove to his favorite pizza place first. He'd placed an order before leaving the parking lot, but he still had to wait for a bit. He'd ordered ten pizzas, and they took a bit to be cooked. It was worth the wait and the bill, though. He loved to see the smile on the kids' faces when he walked into the shelter with his arms full of deliciously smelling boxes.

"I need help," he yelled when he stepped through the shelter door.

The shelter didn't look like much from outside. It blended in with the other houses on the street, except for the flyers stuck on the windows and the small sign that advertised what it was. There was space there for a dozen kids, maybe fifteen if they needed it. Most of them stayed around. It was a safe place for them. No one forced them to do anything, and while Griffith wished he could find loving families for all of them, he understood why he needed to stay out of this. Once the kids trusted him and the others enough, the head of the shelter, Annie, would work with them to help them get back on their feet. Most of the kids had been kicked out of their homes, some beaten and bullied, insulted, torn apart until they didn't know who they could trust — so they didn't trust anyone. The road to recovery was long and hard, but the shelter did everything they could to help, providing a warm place to stay, some privacy, showers, food, and therapy.

That was what the kids needed, and Griffith was grateful he was able to help.

Lindsay's head popped out of the living room. She was seventeen, a short slip of a girl with long, blond hair that swallowed her. She'd been caught kissing her girlfriend a few years back and kicked out by her mom. She'd lived on the streets for a while before Annie had managed to convince her to come to the shelter. Griffith was glad to see she was gaining weight.

"Oh, pizza!" she exclaimed. She rushed toward him and grabbed a few of the boxes. "I'm taking this to the living room to eat with Tay."

"Annie isn't going to be happy that you two are isolating yourselves again."

She bit her lower lip. "He had a bad day."

"Ah." That could mean anything and everything. "All right. I'll tell Annie to give you two some slack, as long as you help with the cleaning up."

Lindsay grinned. "Of course we will." She turned around and rushed back to the living room.

Griffith's heart squeezed with pain. He wanted to give these kids everything they hadn't gotten from their parents, but there was only so much he *could* give them.

He hoped it would be enough.

Lawrence tapped his fingertips on the dining table. He was peering at the file Win had handed off earlier, but he wasn't reading the information there. No, his mind was already on what he'd need to do. "Tomorrow?" he asked.

Win looked like he could sleep a week and still be tired. He rubbed his face and nodded. "Yes. There's no reason to wait, and the sooner we get answers, the better it will be for everyone."

"And you think this Griffith guy has the answers we need?"

"Not him, no, but he's a way to his father."

Lawrence wasn't too sure about that. "Here it says he doesn't visit his parents often."

Win arched a brow. "Because you do?"

Right. "I have a reason not to."

"Maybe, but some of the others find plenty of time to visit family." Win sighed. "But we're not here to talk about you. I know White might not be close to his son. But Griffith White is still his son, and this is the easiest way for us to get info. Even if Griffith doesn't have anything we want, he might be able to help, and we're hoping that his father will give us what we want once he finds out we have him."

Lawrence didn't like this. He didn't like the thought of grabbing someone who hadn't done anything. As far as he could see, Griffith was innocent, and not close to his asshole of a father. Hell, he even worked for Charles Hoffman, a shifter famous for using his wealth to find a way to help the people who'd been hurt in the labs. There was little he could do for people like Lawrence, but he was trying to help, and Lawrence respected that. He also respected that Griffith, a human, was trying to help, too.

He didn't want to kidnap him, but he would. That was his job.

He looked at the picture of Griffith again. He was a good-looking man, in his late twenties, maybe early thirties, with brown eyes and brown hair that looked like he needed a trip to get it cut. Lawrence had expected him to wear glasses, maybe because he was a scientist, but he didn't, and his eyes gleamed, warm and welcoming.

He wasn't going to be welcoming when he saw Lawrence.

"I don't like this."

"I know. I don't either, and Roark and Beck are right there with me. But I talked to the council, and while it's not something we'd normally do, we *need* information on Gavin White, and this is the fastest way. We're already looking into other things, like finding out who he's working with, but that's going to take some time. It's the government we're talking about, and what's more, it's a secret branch of it. Dominic Nash assured me that he trusts his contact in the government, and that person told him that whatever is happening isn't common knowledge and that some of the higher-ups will be furious when they find out."

"You sound sure of that." Lawrence couldn't say he didn't trust humans, but he also wasn't crazy about them, not after what they'd done to him.

"We are. They find us shifters useful. They don't want to jeopardize our place in their army and whatnot. And I trust Dominic and the rest of the council. They're the ones with the contacts, and if they trust them, well, who am I not to?"

Lawrence knew his only job was to obey orders. He liked that Win explained what was happening, though. It made him feel part of something bigger, something that was helping.

He still didn't like the thought of kidnapping an innocent man.

"We could send someone else," Win said.

"We both know I'm the best bet." Because Lawrence could use his venom to knock Griffith out. His venom was lethal if he secreted too much of it, but if he was careful—and he always was—he could knock people out easily. A kiss was enough, and kissing Griffith wouldn't be a hardship.

"You are," Win agreed.

Lawrence would have been glad for any other assignment. He didn't like hanging around the warehouse, not when everyone else was coupled up and all lovey-dovey. He was happy that his friends were happy, but he could do without having to watch them sucking faces. Besides, he wanted this mission to go the right way, and that meant he'd have to do it himself. That way he'd be sure that Griffith wouldn't get hurt. "I'll do it."

Win smiled. "That's what I was hoping you'd say. Thank you, Lawrence."

"Don't thank me. I'm just doing my job. Where am I taking him, then?"

Lawrence, Win, and Roark poured over the plan for several

hours until Lawrence could remember everything by heart. He couldn't fuck this up. He'd never messed up an assignment, and this wasn't the one to start with.

He was relieved when Win and Roark went back to Win's office. He needed some time to think about what he was about to do and what could go wrong. That was the best way to be ready for anything.

He was supposed to take Griffith to a safe house the assassins owned. It was close to where he worked, so Lawrence should be able to get him there easily enough, especially if he could use Griffith's car to get them there. Griffith would be unconscious — that was the first thing Lawrence would do — so Lawrence couldn't carry him around. Griffith wasn't a giant, but Lawrence was on the small side, and even though he was a shifter, it wouldn't have been easy. Besides, people would probably notice something if he had to lug Griffith all the way there.

"You're going out?" Ulric asked when Lawrence joined him. He was behind the stove cooking something. Lawrence leaned closer, wrinkling his nose at the spicy scent that wafted up from the pan.

"Why are you cooking? That's Graham's job."

"Yeah, but I like cooking. So?"

Lawrence rolled his eyes. "Why do you think that? Is it because Win and Roark talked to me and only me for the past two hours? You're a great detective."

Ulric tried to kick Lawrence, but Lawrence moved out of the way. "You're not funny."

"Yeah, I'm going. Tomorrow."

"You know when you'll be back?"

"Nope." Because Lawrence wasn't just supposed to kidnap Griffith. He also had to stay with the guy until he had the answers they needed, and no one could tell how long that was going to be. Beck would take care of contacting Gavin White as soon as Lawrence let him know he had Griffith, but then everything was on that man and out of Lawrence's hands.

He wasn't sure he liked the thought of having to hang around with Griffith, but again, he didn't exactly have a choice. He'd do what he had to.

"It's freaky, huh?" Ulric asked.

"What?"

"Everything. I mean, I thought we were done with this."

"With what? Humans messing with us? That's never going to happen."

"You're probably right." He looked mournful. "But I hate that there's a need for us."

"It's not exactly a need. I mean, if we didn't do this, what could we do? We're freaks of nature now."

Ulric chuckled. "Talk for yourself. I'm perfectly happy with what I am."

"That's because you actually have a cool superpower."

"Being fast is as good as what you can do."

Maybe it was, but it wasn't as alienating as Lawrence's twisted ability. He secreted venom both in his human form and in his snake one, but the scientists who'd worked on him hadn't found a way to make it so that he could get rid of the venom entirely—or they hadn't had the time. There always was a small amount of venom in his system. That meant that he hadn't kissed anyone or let himself get close to anyone ever since he'd realized that. He couldn't afford it. He couldn't *risk* it.

He'd had sex since he'd left the lab, but only rarely, and it was never good because of how careful he had to be. If any of his body fluids entered someone, shifter or human, they could die from it, and he wasn't exactly in control when he was orgasming. That was why he'd decided to stop several years ago, and he didn't regret it. He didn't want to be the reason someone died, not when he hadn't been ordered to.

So sex was out. Kissing was out. He had friends, but sometimes he was still lonely. He longed for a mate, yet he also never wanted to meet him, because what could he give him? They'd never be able to touch or kiss, and that was too much for Lawrence to be able to stand.

No, he was better off on his own.

Griffith still didn't want to go home to his empty apartment, especially after spending the evening with the kids. They were so full of life and noisy, and he wanted to keep that close for another little while. He couldn't stay at the shelter, though. The kids were starting to go to bed, and they needed their privacy.

Griffith ruffled Tay's hair. He and Lindsay had come to the kitchen earlier, and while Lindsay had thrown herself right into the mix, Tay had kept to himself. He usually did, but after what Lindsay had said, Griffith wanted to make sure he was okay. "What's going on?"

Tay rolled his eyes. "I told Lin not to tell you anything."

"She didn't. She just mentioned that you weren't feeling great."

"I'm fine."

"Okay." Tay knew he could talk to Griffith if he wanted or needed to, so Griffith wasn't going to push.

Tay fiddled with the bottom of his pink t-shirt while Griffith stacked the now empty pizza boxes. The other kids had disappeared, and Annie was in her office, doing whatever she always did. Griffith loved volunteering there, but he wouldn't know where to start if he were in charge. Luckily for everyone involved, he wasn't.

"It's just . . . how do you know what you are?" Tay asked.

Griffith smiled. He'd hoped Tay would feel comfortable enough to talk to him.

"What do you mean?"

Tay wasn't looking at Griffith. "Like, I know I'm a guy be-cause I was born that way."

"That's not true, and you know that, too."

Tay smiled. "Yeah. But what I mean is, I have, you know, I'm a guy down there, and that's okay. But I don't *feel* like a guy."

Griffith knew he needed to be careful. He wasn't a thera-pist, so he wasn't sure how much he could help Tay. He wanted to try, though. "What do you feel like?"

"That's the thing. I'm not sure. I don't feel like a guy, but I also don't think I'm a girl. I don't feel like anything. I just like what I like."

"You're talking about clothes and accessories?"

"Yeah. I don't like skirts, but I like this t-shirt. You know what I mean?"

Griffith thought he did. Tay was wearing a pink shirt that was probably from the women's section of whatever store he'd found it at. Griffith could tell by the cut. Tay was also wearing jeans and yellow socks, several bracelets on both his wrists and a hint of lipstick. He was a joyful mix of male and female. "You know you can be what you want to be," Griffith began. He wasn't sure that *want* was the right word, but he wanted Tay to know he was accepted the way he was.

"Yeah, I know. But what *am* I?"

"Does it really matter? I understand where you're coming from only in part. I've always felt like a guy. But you're Tay. You like what you like. Maybe you're a guy, maybe you're a girl, or maybe you're genderless. That's okay, too. You're only seventeen, and you have all the time in the world to find your label, if that's what you want. No one here cares about it. We only care about *you*."

Tay's smile widened. "I know. I'm just trying to figure my-self out, you know?"

"I know. Everyone is trying to do the same at seventeen. I'm glad you talked to me, although I'm not sure how much I helped."

Griffith left the shelter with his heart full. God, he wanted to adopt all those kids, bring them home and protect them from the world that already had hurt them so much. He still didn't want to go home, even though it was going on ten PM, so he headed to his grandfather's house instead.

He was always welcome there. His grandfather hated the way his daughter was treated by her husband as much as Griffith did, which was why he wasn't welcome in her home anymore. He didn't have a problem telling Griffith's father what he thought of him, and Griffith loved him for that. He'd been like a second, better father to him, pushing him into following his dreams when he was still a kid rather than following his father's orders. Griffith's life would have been very different if he'd done what his father asked of him instead of listening to his grandfather.

"Anyone home?" he asked as he pushed the door open. He had a key for when his grandfather needed him to feed his cats and water his plants.

One of the cats, a white Persian named Persephone, came rushing and tried to sneak past Griffith's legs. He grabbed her and hauled her up. "Jesus, girl. I thought you were all fluff and hair, but you're heavy."

Persephone glared at Griffith until he put her down. Then she slunk away, her tail held high in affront, either at his words or at the fact that he'd dared stop her in her dash for freedom. She probably wouldn't have gone far—she was an inside cat through and through—but the last thing Griffith needed right now was to spend half the night outside in his grandfather's extensive garden looking for her.

"Anyone home?" he called out again, even though he'd seen the light was on in the living room.

Griffith had never understood how his grandfather could live alone in such a big house. More than a house, it was a mansion, and while he did have help with the cleaning and general upkeep, he was the only one who lived there. Sometimes Griffith wondered if maybe he should move in with his grandfather, just to keep an eye on him. His grandfather would have been horrified at the thought that he might need a keeper, but he wasn't getting any younger, and Griffith was terrified of losing him.

"What are you doing here? Nothing better to do than to visit me?" his grandfather asked when Griffith walked into the living room. He was sitting in front of the empty fireplace, a bottle of water on the small table next to his armchair, a book in his lap, his feet propped up on an ottoman.

Griffith flopped into the armchair in front of his grandfather's. "Not really."

"No date?"

"You know better than to ask that."

Griffith's grandfather sighed. "I do, but there's more to life than work, Griff."

"I'm aware of that. I was at the shelter earlier."

"I meant a man. You need love in your life."

"If I'm going to end up like Mom, I'd rather be alone." Griffith liked that he didn't have to watch what he said when he was with his grandfather, but he didn't like the sadness his words created in the old man.

"You're nothing like your mother. You're strong, and the day a man tells you what to do and you obey is the day I'll die."

Griffith smiled. "Damn right. But you know how little time I have."

"I do, but you have to make time for your private life, Griff. What you're doing, both with your job and with those kids, is great and exactly what I hoped you would end up doing when you were a kid, but it's not enough. Humans need love."

"I *have* love. I have you, and the kids at the shelter."

Griffith's grandfather just smiled in answer. Griffith knew he wasn't wrong—there was a reason he hadn't gone home after leaving the shelter. He liked his apartment, but he didn't like how empty it always was. He'd thought about getting a pet, but it wouldn't be fair, because he was never home. He kept himself busy to avoid that.

Maybe things would be different if he dated, but how was he supposed to do that when he had the example of how bad things could go? He knew he wasn't his mother, but that didn't help as much as he wished it did.

Maybe if he found out he had a mate.

He knew mates weren't perfect, that they could hurt their mates just as much as husbands could, but he'd seen enough mated couples in his work to know how much love there could be between them, too. *That* was what he wanted. He wanted someone who would accept him the way he was, who wouldn't try to change him or to control him. He wanted someone who would come with him to the shelter instead of trying to get him to go home and leave the kids behind.

The fact that if he was someone's mate meant that he'd be with a shifter and that his father would be furious was a bonus.

CHAPTER TWO

Lawrence was as ready as he'd ever be.

He always felt that way before a mission—never ready enough, yet he knew it would have to do. And that was okay. He knew what he had to do, and he would do it, no matter how little he liked it.

"Ready?" Dasha asked.

They were already in the room dedicated to shimmering. It was little more than a closet, big enough only for a few people, but then Dasha usually only shimmered with one assassin at a time. When he had to come and go with a group, he used the garage.

"Yeah."

Dasha held out a hand and smiled. "Let's go, then."

Lawrence took the offered hand. He didn't even have time to close his eyes before Dasha shimmered them away and into a parking garage. He'd chosen a hidden spot by the stairs, and since it was so late at night, the garage was empty. There were still a few cars parked there, and Lawrence immediately spotted Griffith White's.

Beck had done his homework, so Lawrence knew what Griffith drove, where he lived, what he did for a living, and even that he often visited a shelter for LGBTQ human teenagers. The man sounded too good to be true, especially with what Lawrence knew about his father. But the proof was there, and Lawrence couldn't deny that Griffith White looked like a good guy on paper. The thought of having to kidnap him was abhorrent, but it was what Lawrence had to do, and he'd do it. That was his job, and Win hadn't been wrong when he'd said that the council and all the shifters and other paranormal beings they represented needed answers to questions they couldn't openly ask.

"Everything good?" Dasha asked in a whisper.

Lawrence nodded. "You can go."

"All right. Stay safe."

Dasha disappeared, and Lawrence focused on Griffith White's car. He knew White always stayed at work until late, which was why he'd decided to do this here. The place was deserted, and with Beck taking care of the security cameras, this should be an easy in and out job.

Lawrence didn't have to wait long. He heard the elevator ping and its door slide open from where he was. He stayed still, watching a man he recognized from Griffith White's pictures walk out. He wasn't paying attention to what he was doing, because he was reading a file. His car keys were in his hand, and a messenger bag hung from his shoulder.

Lawrence moved when White stopped in front of his car. White put the files he was still holding on top of the car and unlocked it. The beep was loud in the parking lot, and its echo masked the sound Lawrence made when he approached. "Excuse me?"

White visibly startled. He dropped his keys to the ground, and he twirled around, pressing his back against his car. Lawrence saw the moment he took him in and relaxed. Everyone always relaxed when they saw Lawrence. He knew why—he was short, just five feet five, and he looked innocent. His blond hair and blue eyes helped with that impression, and he cultivated it because it helped with his job. No one ever suspected him of being able to hurt them when they saw him.

"Yes?" White asked. He pushed himself away from his car.

Lawrence smiled as sweetly as he could. "My car won't start." He gestured toward one of the few other cars that were still there.

"Oh. I'm sorry about that. How can I help?"

"I was wondering if you could give me a ride. I already called for someone to come look at it, but they won't be able to do that until tomorrow, and I have no idea how to get home, because my phone died." Lawrence played up the innocent vampy part he could act so well. He'd had plenty of occasions to get perfect at it.

White looked around, hesitant. "I could loan you my phone so you can call someone. Your girlfriend, maybe?"

Lawrence giggled. God, he hated giggling. "I don't have a girlfriend or a boyfriend. I don't have anyone to call." He moved closer. When White didn't react to that, Lawrence smiled even wider and put a hand on White's arm. "Please? I promise I'll be nice if you help me."

White blinked. "Nice?"

"You can take what you want from that." Lawrence fluttered his lashes.

"I — all right."

There it was. Lawrence pressed his front against White and kissed him. White's eyes and lips widened in shock, and Lawrence took advantage of it. He slipped his tongue into White's mouth to make sure enough of his saliva entered the man's system.

Then it hit him, when White slumped against him, unconscious. Lawrence had been so focused on what he was doing that he hadn't smelled it. The smells of the garage also didn't help, but now that Griffith White was slumped over Lawrence, there was no way Lawrence could have ignored it.

"Shit. Fuck. Fuck!" Lawrence muttered as he pushed Griffith away. He lowered him to the ground and quickly grabbed his keys. The car was already unlocked, so he walked around the car to open the passenger seat, then he went back to grab Griffith.

He still smelled like Lawrence's mate when Lawrence hauled him up.

"For fuck's sake. What the fuck is happening?" Lawrence muttered. He was lucky he was a shifter, because he doubted he'd have managed to carry his mate around the car otherwise. Griffith was only six inches taller than Lawrence, but he was larger, and while Lawrence couldn't wait to see what was hiding under his clothes, now wasn't the moment.

He dumped Griffith into the passenger seat and buckled him in. When he walked to the driver side, he grabbed the files and the messenger bag that had fallen to the ground and threw them in the back seat as he slipped behind the wheel. He slammed the door shut and took a moment to breathe.

This wasn't how things were supposed to go. Griffith wasn't supposed to be Lawrence's mate. He was supposed to be Gavin White's son, nothing more, nothing less.

But he wasn't.

"For fuck's sake." Lawrence started the car and left the garage. It was almost eleven PM, and the streets were empty. Lawrence didn't worry about the cameras that would no doubt film him in Griffith's car. Beck would make sure no one ever found out about this, and considering that Griffith was Lawrence's mate, Lawrence doubted Griffith would mind.

Of course, that was if Griffith wanted Lawrence in his life. Griffith was a good guy, no matter who his father was or what he'd done. Lawrence, not so much.

Lawrence was a killer. It was what he'd been created to be. He'd tried to go back home after he'd been released from the lab where he'd been kept, but he hadn't been able to get used to his old life again. It made sense—he hadn't been the old him anymore. But this new him, the him who seduced and killed people with a kiss, was a killer, and Griffith was very much not. He was a lover, as his work with the kids in the shelter showed.

Lawrence didn't know what to do about this. The easy way was to follow the orders he'd gotten, the plans he'd set up, so he did. He couldn't stop thinking about Griffith, though, about what would happen when he woke up. Lawrence was going to have to explain what was going on, and he wasn't looking forward to it. He also didn't want to use the fact that they were mates to get the answers he needed from Griffith and his father.

Griffith wouldn't know they were mates until Lawrence told him. Maybe he'd see the fact that Lawrence would keep it a secret from him like a betrayal, but that was the best way to do things. Once Lawrence and the council had what they needed, Lawrence could tell Griffith they were mates and see what happened.

Lawrence drove to the council's safe house. It was furnished, so Griffith would be comfortable there. He wasn't a prisoner, even though Lawrence realized how bad things would look when Griffith woke up. He was going to have to tie Griffith up, at least in the beginning, just to make sure he wouldn't try to escape before Lawrence could tell him what was going on.

Lawrence wasn't sure that was something they'd be able to come back from, but he supposed he was going to find out soon enough.

Griffith jerked awake and started panicking as soon as he opened his eyes.

He pulled on his arm and realized he was tied to the bed where he was stretched out. He didn't recognize the room he was in, and since the last thing he could remember was that cute little guy kissing him, he knew he was right to be freaking out.

That didn't mean he liked it. He *hated* it. He should have

enough state of mind to keep calm and try to find a way out instead of giving in to the panic. That wasn't going to help him at all.

He tried to breathe. He was unharmed, and nothing hurt, so maybe things weren't as bad as he'd initially thought. Maybe there *was* a way out of this. He just needed to find it.

"Hey. You're awake."

Griffith rolled his head on the pillow to look at the man who'd talked. It was the cutie who'd kissed him, and he was carrying a tray with food on it. Griffith couldn't see what that food was from the bed, but the air smelled like fries, and his stomach grumbled. He wasn't sure he'd eaten lunch, and he had no idea what time it was.

The man came closer and put the tray onto the nightstand next to the bed. Griffith stayed still, not sure what to expect. The man looked sweet and adorable, but his actions didn't match with his appearance. "Who are you?" Griffith spat out. He hoped the fear he felt wasn't apparent in his voice.

The man bit his lower lip, and for fuck's sake, could anyone look cuter? "I'm sorry I had to do this."

"Had to? You didn't *have* to do anything. You didn't have to — to kidnap me? Why the fuck did you do that?" Maybe this guy wanted his grandfather's money. He was wealthy, very much so, so it was possible.

The man cleared his throat. "I'm Lawrence."

"Do I look like I care?"

Lawrence jerked back. It was almost as if he was hurt by Griffith's question, and probably his tone of voice. Griffith wasn't supposed to care, but for some reason, he did.

"Are you going to run if I untie you?" Lawrence asked.

Griffith knew he should, but somehow, he doubted he could. Lawrence might look all sweet and whatnot, but he'd managed to knock Griffith out, and Griffith still had no idea how he'd managed.

"No."

Lawrence cocked his head.

He probably didn't believe Griffith. Griffith didn't think he'd have believed himself in Lawrence's place. He sighed. "Why don't you tell me why you kidnapped me? You want money?"

"No."

"What, then?" Griffith couldn't think about anything else.

Lawrence gestured to Griffith's hand. "I'll untie you. Then we'll talk. I just need you to listen to me, okay? I promise I won't hurt you."

"And I'm supposed to believe that?"

"I could have hurt you while you were unconscious. I didn't."

That much was true. Griffith didn't believe Lawrence was a vulnerable cutie anymore. "All right. Let's say I believe you and that you believe I won't try to run."

Lawrence smiled again, and good God, how was Griffith supposed to want to leave? He'd never been one for looks, not in his boyfriends, but he suspected there was a lot more to Lawrence than this, and for some reason, he wanted to find out what it was. Lawrence quickly untied Griffith. Griffith flexed his wrist, but it didn't hurt. The restraints hadn't been tight enough to do that.

"You should eat," Lawrence said.

Griffith sat up—a burger and fries. His stomach growled again, but he didn't reach for the food. "I want answers."

"And I'll give them to you, as long as you eat. You're hungry, aren't you? I didn't drug the food, I promise. I wouldn't have to, to make sure you don't leave."

Griffith had no problem believing that. He grabbed the tray without looking away from Lawrence. Lawrence sat at the foot of the bed, far enough away that they didn't touch. Griffith was strangely sorry about that, but he didn't allow himself to dwell on that. "Why did you take me?" he asked before biting into the burger.

"The people I work for need answers."

"Answers?"

Lawrence sighed. "I don't know how much you know about your father's job."

Griffith blinked. This wasn't what he'd expected at all. "My father?" This wasn't about money, then.

"Yes. Do you know who he works for? *What* his job consists of?"

"He works for the government. He's a scientist." Pretty much like Griffith was, except he worked for gain while Griffith was trying to help people who'd been wronged.

"He is. Did you know he's experimenting on shifters again?"

Griffith's stomach turned to ice. "What?" he croaked, suddenly not hungry anymore.

"He's working for the government. He has their approval to experiment on shifters. We don't know who exactly is involved, how many shifters, what kind, or even where they're kept. That's what we have to find out."

"And you thought I could give you the answers?" Griffith felt like he was going to puke. He knew his father wasn't a good man. He'd always known that, but he hadn't realized his father's hate went that deep. He had no problem believing that his father had a hand in this, though. He didn't want to, didn't want the man he'd grown up with to be a monster, but there was no denying it, and Griffith wasn't going to hide his head in the sand.

He swallowed. "What do you want from me?"

"To get those answers from your father."

Griffith snorted. "He's never going to give them to me. I'm not even supposed to know about this. I *don't* know about this. He doesn't talk to me about his job. He doesn't like that

I refused to work with him and went to work for a shifter instead." It made sense, didn't it? His father hated shifters, and Griffith worked for one. His father hated gays, and Griffith was one.

"Then we're going to use you as leverage."

It took Griffith a moment to catch on to what Lawrence was saying.

Then he laughed. He couldn't stop laughing. His stomach hurt, and he pressed his hand against it. He knew the way he was behaving was mostly from shock, but the thought that his father would give a shit about him, enough that he'd give Lawrence and whoever he worked for the answers they wanted, was ridiculous.

"Griffith?"

Griffith hadn't told Lawrence his name, but of course he knew it. He seemed to know a lot about Griffith, except the most crucial part. "My father isn't going to tell you anything."

"We have you."

"And he won't give a shit. He hates me."

Lawrence frowned. "Why?"

"Why not? He hates anyone who isn't like him. And by that, I mean everyone who isn't a white human heterosexual male. I work for a shifter, and I'm gay. He's never accepted either of those. He's not going to try to rescue me. Hell, he's probably going to be happy to learn I'm not going to be a problem anymore. He might even tell you to kill me, for all he cares. There's no love lost between us, trust me. You're not going to get anything from him, not even using me. Hell, you wouldn't get anything even if you used my mother, and they've been married for close to thirty years."

Lawrence exhaled. His shoulders slumped, and to Griffith's surprise, he smiled. "That both complicates things and makes them easier."

"How? I couldn't help you." But Griffith wanted to. He

wasn't surprised at what his father was doing, and now that he knew, he wanted to help stop him. He *needed* to help because even though this wasn't his fault, he felt responsible.

He should have known his father would do something like this. His father thought shifters were animals, and he had no problem experimenting on animals. Griffith had always hated his father's point of view, but he'd never thought things would get this far.

"I'll get back to you about that. I need to make a phone call."

"Who are you working for, Lawrence?" Griffith had a pretty good idea, but he wanted to be sure.

Lawrence hesitated. "I suppose you're going to find out sooner or later, considering everything. I work for the council."

"The shifter council."

Lawrence smiled. "Is there another one? Yes, for them."

It made sense. They'd want the shifters to be free and safe, and Griffith wanted the same thing. "I want to help."

Lawrence had to call Win. What Griffith had told him changed everything, maybe as much as the fact that they were mates — or more. Lawrence wasn't sure of anything anymore, and he was glad he wouldn't be the one making decisions in this case.

"You're leaving?" Griffith asked.

Lawrence didn't want to. He could tell Griffith was freaking out, although he wasn't sure if it was because he'd woken up tied to a bed in a place he didn't know or because of what he'd been told about his father. "I'm only going to the next room. I promise I'm not leaving you." Should Lawrence tell him that they were mates? Would he believe him if he did, though? Or would he think Lawrence was saying that only because he wanted him to trust him?

Lawrence needed to talk to Win first. Win was going to have an opinion about how to deal with this, and Lawrence would be more than happy to follow his lead. He had no idea what to do, and for the first time in forever, the thought of making a decision—possibly the wrong one—terrified him.

Griffith looked around. "Is there anyone else here?"

"No. We're alone." That sounded creepy, didn't it? "I promise I won't hurt you."

To Lawrence's surprise, Griffith smiled. "I know."

Lawrence wanted to ask how he could possibly know, but he *really* had to make that phone call. He had no idea if Win and Roark had a secondary plan for this or if they were going to have to wing it. He wanted to strangle—or better, poison—Gavin White himself for what Griffith had told him, but that wasn't his place.

He was relieved Griffith and his father didn't get along, though. There was no denying that. Gavin White was a monster, and Lawrence would have been distraught to find out his mate was, too. Not that it changed anything, not when Lawrence would never be able to even kiss Griffith.

That was why he couldn't tell him about their bond. He was going to have to tell Win, but it would be better if Griffith never found out. That way, he'd be able to get back out there, maybe meet a man and marry the guy. Lawrence already hated his guts for being able to have what he couldn't, but while he was destined to a future alone, Griffith wasn't. This had to be done, no matter how little Lawrence liked it.

He left Griffith to his burger, closing the bedroom door but not locking it, and went to the living room. The house was empty and sparsely furnished, only enough to be comfortable. There were no personal items because it wasn't anyone's home. It was a place where the assassins could stay if they needed it, be it because a job had gone wrong or because they had to stick around for whatever reason. It was surprisingly dust free, and while the fridge was empty, the pantry was stocked. Lawrence doubted he and Griffith would stay there long, though. There was only one reason he'd been sent to retrieve Griffith, and that was to get answers about his father and to use him as leverage. Since that was out, Griffith could go back to his life made of a good job helping shifters and shelter kids.

"You already have the answers we need?" Win asked when he answered the phone after only one ring.

"No. What I have is a problem. Actually, make that two."

"What is it? Do you need me to send someone to help you?"

Lawrence sighed. He flopped onto the couch and closed his eyes, tilting his face toward the ceiling. "No. I'm safe, and so is Griffith. We're not going to be able to use him to get what we want from his father, though. From what Griffith told me, his father is the kind of person who hates anyone who's not like him. That includes shifters, but also his son."

"Why?"

"Griffith is gay. That's not a good thing in White's world."

"Somehow, I'm not surprised."

Lawrence wasn't, either. "That means that White isn't going to give us shit."

Win sighed so loudly that Lawrence heard him. "That's what I thought. And Griffith doesn't know anything at all about his father's job?"

"No. He was horrified when I told him what we knew. He wants to help, but he doesn't know how. He can't tell us anything."

"And now he knows we're investigating his father, and he's seen your face."

"Yeah. I don't think he's going to create problems, though. As I said, he wants to help, even though he doesn't know how."

"I understand that, but it's still his father we're talking about. It can't be easy to actively go against him, even though Griffith knows what his father is doing."

"He wants to do right by shifters, though. You know that. He chose a job where he could help us." That didn't mean he was a good guy, but Lawrence needed to believe it, even though he wasn't planning on telling Griffith about their bond.

"I know that. I'm still not sure that involving him in this is a good idea. What we need is information, and if he can't help with that, what can he do?"

Lawrence sucked in a breath. "There's more."

"Dammit. Of course there is. There *always* is. What is it?"

"He's my mate."

Win was silent for so long that Lawrence wondered what he was thinking. Finding your mate was usually a happy event, although Win knew Lawrence well enough to realize that he was probably conflicted about it.

And he was. He wanted Griffith. He wanted a life with him, the way North was with Milo, Win with Graham. He wanted that more than he could explain, but he'd known he couldn't have it since he'd been freed from the lab and discovered what he could do. He couldn't put anyone's life in danger, least of all his mate's. If that meant he'd be alone for the rest of his life, that he'd have to watch Griffith fall in love with someone else and be happy with them, then so be it.

"I'm not sure what to tell you," Win finally said.

"I know."

"I'm happy for you, but . . ."

"I know." Win was aware of what Lawrence's ability meant. He knew that was the reason Lawrence didn't date—although being an assassin didn't help, either.

Win huffed. "All right. What do you want to do?"

"What are the options?" And why was Win asking Lawrence what he wanted to do when he wasn't the one in charge?

"Well, you could take Griffith home and hope he forgets everything that happened tonight. I'm not saying you wouldn't be able to see him again, but that's on you. It'll be a personal decision."

"Or?" Lawrence suspected what Win was about to say, and he knew he wouldn't like it.

"Or he could help us. I know you're not going to like this, but even though he doesn't know much about what his father does, he could find out. If he wants to help us, he'll be more than welcome to."

Lawrence sighed. "He's going to want to." He'd just met Griffith, but he could tell. Griffith was a helper, and now that he knew that his father was involved in hurting shifters, he'd probably do whatever he could to neutralize him. He wouldn't understand exactly what that meant in the beginning, but if he was on board, Win would explain to him. He'd have a choice.

He already did, and Lawrence couldn't take it from him. It wouldn't be fair. "I'll talk to him and see what he wants to do."

"Good. Since Griffith doesn't think his father will give us what we want through blackmail, we won't send him the message that we have his son. This way, Griffith should be able to go home to him and ask questions without having him suspect that something is up."

The thought of having Griffith face his father like that made Lawrence's stomach churn, but he didn't say anything. It wasn't his decision. It was Win's, and Roark's. Not Lawrence's.

"He's going to want to help," Lawrence said.

"Good. I'm sending Dasha to you."

"You want me to take him to the warehouse?" It made sense, but Lawrence had a hard time imagining Griffith there, in the place he considered home.

Griffith was going to dig himself a place in Lawrence's life whether Lawrence liked it or not, wasn't he? He was going to embed himself there, and Lawrence would have to learn to deal with it.

Griffith knew he should probably be afraid. No matter what Lawrence had told him, what he'd explained, he'd still kidnapped Griffith. That wasn't something people did.

Yet Griffith didn't feel that fear. Hell, he even *liked* Lawrence, which was just as crazy as the rest of the evening had been.

And what his father was doing. God, Griffith was horrified by that. He'd known his father was a bad man, an asshole, but he'd never thought things would come to this. He was experimenting on shifters. He was hurting people, human beings, and he was not one bit repentant about it. What was Griffith supposed to do with that knowledge? There was no way he'd ever be able to look his father in the eye again and not tell him what he thought of him. He knew that trying to change his father's mind wouldn't work, and that was okay. He wasn't even going to try.

"Can I come in?" Lawrence asked.

Griffith hadn't heard him come back, yet he was standing behind the door. "Of course." He'd finished his burger and the fries, and he felt better, less off-kilter. Knowing that Lawrence was after his father rather than him also had helped, even though Griffith was more confused than ever now.

Lawrence walked in. "All right, I talked to my boss."

Griffith perked up. He wanted to ask about a hundred questions—who was Lawrence, who did he work for, what did he do except for kidnapping people, what were he and his colleagues going to do to stop his father, and more importantly, what could he do to help — but he pressed his lips together. Lawrence looked a bit overwhelmed, and Griffith didn't want to make things worse. "And?" was all he asked.

Lawrence hesitated. "He'd like for you to help if you're okay with it. Since we can't get answers by using the leverage of having you with us, we need to find another way to get them."

"I can ask him." Griffith wasn't sure he'd get them, and at the very least, his father would be suspicious, but maybe Griffith could fake admitting to him that he wasn't happy with his job, or maybe that he wanted to earn more money. He wasn't sure his father would believe him, but he needed to do something, and this was what he could think of. "When do you want me to go?"

Lawrence shook his head. "You're not going anywhere right now. My boss wants to talk to you, and that means you're coming with me, unless you'd rather back off and go your own way. That's okay, too. It's probably the safer option."

That sounded like Lawrence was trying to dissuade Griffith from coming. Griffith wasn't sure why, but he wasn't going to say yes. "I want to help," he repeated.

Lawrence sighed. "That's what I was afraid of. Okay, someone is coming to pick us up. Your car will be safe here, so that's not a worry, and we can either send someone to grab some of your stuff from your apartment, or you can go with them once you and Win have talked and you've decided what you want to do."

Griffith blinked. "You mean I'm going to stay with you?"

"I don't know. I'm not the one in charge."

Griffith put the tray back onto the nightstand. "Let's go, then." He stopped and grabbed the tray again. "Just let me clean up first."

Lawrence laughed. Griffith hadn't expected it, and he smiled in answer.

"All right, you can clean up. I'm sure the next person who uses the house will be happy you did."

Griffith had so *many* questions. He hoped Lawrence's boss, whoever he was, would answer at least some of them.

There wasn't much to clean up. Griffith threw away the burger wrapper and the fry container, washed his hands, and straightened the blanket on the bed. That was it. He still didn't know what time it was, but when he left the bedroom, he found Lawrence in the living room, his messenger bag and the files he'd been reading when he'd left work on the coffee table. His cell phone was there as well, although it was shut off. He reached toward it, but he didn't take it. "Can I turn it back on?"

"I'd rather you didn't, not yet. Once we're home, you can ask our IT guy to make sure no one will be able to find you using it. In the meantime, it's better you don't. We need to keep the place where we live a secret."

Griffith sat on the edge of the couch. "Can I ask you something?"

"You can ask, but I can't promise I'll answer."

"You're a shifter, right? I mean, you said you were here on behalf of the council."

"I am."

"What kind? Or is that rude to ask?" Griffith might work for shifters, help them, but he didn't have a lot of contact with them, or even with humans. His work happened in a lab, not with people.

"Snake."

"Oh." That didn't tell Griffith much, but it was a start.

"Are you afraid now? Disgusted?"

Griffith blinked. "No. Why should I?"

Lawrence shrugged. "I don't know. People don't usually like snakes."

"But you're not just a snake, are you? You're also human. Besides, I'm not afraid of snakes. Insects, on the other hand, freak me out, so I'd probably have run away if you'd told me you were a spider shifter."

"I don't think those exist."

"Thank God. The more legs they have, the more horrible they are. Snakes, though? I like snakes." Even though he hadn't actually ever touched one. The closest he'd come was watching snakes behind the glass at the reptile house, but Lawrence didn't need to know that.

Griffith wasn't sure whether he was relieved or annoyed when a man with blond hair appeared in the corner of the room. He had green eyes and pointed ears, so Griffith didn't have to ask to know what he was—as if the shimmering hadn't been enough.

"Hey, Dasha," Lawrence said, turning his attention to the newcomer.

Griffith frowned. He didn't like it. He wanted Lawrence's attention on him. He was clearly more tired than he'd thought, and from what he could understand, his day wasn't over yet. He was going to be a mess tomorrow morning.

"Will I be able to go to work tomorrow?" he asked. He hadn't thought about it until now, but he couldn't just stop going.

"I don't know. You can ask Win what he wants to do when you see him, though."

"Win? Is that your boss?"

Lawrence hesitated. Griffith didn't like seeing him like that, especially when he'd been the one to make him uncomfortable. Hopefully, he'd get the answers he wanted soon, and Lawrence could stop thinking about every word that came out of his mouth.

Griffith put his hands up. "Okay, I get it. You don't know what you can or can't talk about. Let's go meet this boss of yours. You'll be able to relax then."

Griffith grabbed his bag from the coffee table. He didn't miss the puzzled glance Dasha gave Lawrence, but no one said anything. Griffith came to stand in front of Dasha, but that was when things became awkward. "I've never shimmered before," he confessed.

Dasha's smile was warm. "That's all right. There's not much to it. Just take my hand, maybe close your eyes so you won't feel dizzy, and we can go."

"I know it's that easy, of course." Griffith took Dasha's offered hand and closed his eyes. "It's a bit weird, though, you know? I mean, the thought of being here one second and who knows how many miles away the next is unsettling. Although I guess you wouldn't know. You were born with this ability. *I* have to seem strange to you."

"Do you always babble when you're nervous?" Lawrence asked. He sounded amused.

"Pretty much. It's a way to avoid thinking about the thing that's making me nervous. Trust me, I get bad if I don't distract myself."

"You don't have to be nervous."

"Of course you'd say that. I bet you've shimmered hundreds of times already."

"Open your eyes, Griffith."

Griffith cracked one eye open. He'd expected to still be in the living room, but he should have known better.

The three of them were in a small room. There was nothing in it, no furniture, but it was clean, and the door was open. "Are we there?" He didn't know where there was, but the shimmering was over, and he hadn't felt anything.

Lawrence smiled. "We are. See? It wasn't that bad, was it?"

"I didn't even realize."

Dasha dropped Griffith's hand. "Welcome, and I'll see you later."

Griffith hoped he would. He was curious, and he wasn't eager to leave Lawrence behind and to go back to his old, boring life.

CHAPTER THREE

Lawrence could tell Griffith was impressed as he led him up the stairs to the kitchen. He wasn't sure why Win wanted to meet Griffith there rather than in his office, but who was he to argue? That wasn't his job. He was just one of the assassins. Even the fact that Griffith was his mate didn't matter, not when he wasn't going to tell him.

"What is this place?" Griffith asked in a whisper when Lawrence opened the door to the kitchen.

He supposed he was lucky that only a few people were there. He didn't know where everyone else was, and he didn't want to find out. In bed, probably.

And that reminded him—where was Griffith going to sleep? Would he stay at the warehouse, or would Dasha take him back to his apartment? Lawrence wasn't sure what he wanted. On the one hand, he wanted Griffith close, even though nothing would happen between them. On the other hand, having Griffith back home where he couldn't see him would no doubt help Lawrence get over him. His snake wasn't happy with that, but it did realize that being together would put Griffith's life in jeopardy, and if there was one thing Lawrence and the snake agreed on, it was that Griffith had to be kept safe at all costs.

"Welcome. I'm Win." Win said as he looked up. He was sitting at the dining table with Roark and Beck, their heads close together as they planned whatever it was they were planning. Notebooks and files were strewn all over the table, and to Lawrence's surprise, they didn't try to cover them or remove them when Griffith got closer. They were behaving as if Griffith and Lawrence would eventually end up together, and Lawrence didn't know what to do with that.

"Uh, hello. I'm Griffith."

Win smiled. "We know. Why don't you sit down? Have you eaten? Because if you haven't, my mate made lasagna for dinner, and there are leftovers."

"Of course he made lasagna," Lawrence grumbled. "Why does he always do it when I'm not home?"

Win chuckled. "He doesn't do it on purpose, and like I said, there are leftovers."

"We already ate, but thank you," Griffith said. He widened his eyes at Lawrence in an obvious attempt to make him shut up, and it hit Lawrence right in the chest.

They were already behaving as if they were together, weren't they? At least in some ways, like Griffith had just done.

Win cleared his throat. "I'd like to apologize for what happened tonight."

Griffith smiled. "You mean the kidnapping? Don't worry, I'm already over it."

"That's . . . I'll admit, I didn't expect you to take this so well."

Griffith sat on one of the empty chairs. He looked tired, but Lawrence didn't think he'd accept delaying this meeting until tomorrow. Besides, they *all* looked tired. They *were* tired. They hadn't been getting a lot of sleep lately, with all the drama and the problems, especially Win, Roark, and Beck. Being in charge sucked, and Lawrence was glad he just had to follow orders.

Griffith leaned back in the chair. "Well, I can't say I wasn't freaking out when I first woke up. I had no idea where I was or how I'd ended up there. I mean, when I first saw Lawrence, I thought we might end up in bed, but I certainly didn't expect

41

to be *tied* to it."

Dammit. Lawrence could feel his cheeks heating.

He sat next to Griffith, hoping to distract everyone enough that they wouldn't notice how flustered he was.

They all laughed. Lawrence didn't, but he could see the humor in the situation.

Griffith sobered up. "So I was scared, yes, but then Lawrence explained why he'd taken me, and I became horrified. You have to believe that I had no idea what my father was doing. I know he's not a good man, and that his ethics leave a lot to be desired, but I never thought he'd do something like this. I've been working for years to try to find a way to undo the damage, or at least some of the damage, that was done to shifters and humans by the Glass Research Company. I'd like to say I can't believe my father could hurt people, but actually, I can. It's exactly the kind of things he might do. I didn't think he'd push himself that far, or maybe didn't want to believe it, but it does fit what I know about him."

"We don't think you had anything to do with it," Win reassured. "The reason we got you rather than him is that we thought we might be able to influence him by having you."

"And like I told Lawrence, you can't. My father probably won't care if I disappear, and even if he does, there's nothing as important to him as his job, especially not his gay son. I have two things going against me in his eyes, the fact that I'm gay, and my job. You won't get anything using me as leverage, and I don't have anything to tell you, because I didn't know about this until now."

"Is there anything you can do?" Roark asked. Griffith blinked at him, and Roark smiled. "Right, sorry. I'm Roark, and this is Beck."

"Nice to meet you, and I don't know. I'd like to say there is, but like I already told you, my relationship with my father is anything but easy. I do want to try, though. I was thinking about maybe telling him that I'm not happy with my job anymore. He's always wanted me to work with him. He was over the moon when I went into the same area of study, but when I chose to work for a shifter, well, I'll let you imagine what his reaction was."

"And you think he'll believe you're regretting it?"

Lawrence didn't like this plan. From what he knew of Gavin White and what Griffith had told him about the guy, there was no way things would go smoothly. Gavin White was a cruel asshole, and Lawrence doubted he'd stop just because the person in front of him was his son. No, sending Griffith into the thick of things was a bad idea.

But Lawrence couldn't stop him, could he? He might be able to if he told Griffith they were mates, but something told him Griffith wouldn't heed his warnings anyway. He wanted to help, that much was obvious. He wanted his father to pay for what he was doing. Lawrence doubted Griffith would stop, even if it was in the face of danger.

"I don't know. I have no idea if I'm a good actor, but I don't see another way to get the answers you need unless you can hack into his computer or something."

"I might be able to if I had it," Beck said, but everyone in the room knew that would be almost impossible.

"Maybe you can send Dasha to steal it," Lawrence suggested. Anything to keep Griffith safe.

"That's certainly something we can do, and probably the safest for everyone involved. It wouldn't be a bad thing if Griffith tried to get answers, though," Win said.

Goddammit. Win knew Griffith was Lawrence's mate. Why was he doing this to him?

"I suggest everyone go to bed now," Roark said, getting up and stretching. "We're tired, and it's late. We can regroup tomorrow morning and go over this again, once we've had time to think."

"Uh, what about me? Am I going home? Because I have no idea where I am," Griffith said.

"You can ask Dasha to shimmer you home if you find him, but maybe it would be easier if you stayed, take tomorrow off? You could blame a stomach bug or something. That way, we'll have all the time we need to talk this over again, and you'll be able to sleep for as long as you need."

Lawrence was all for keeping Griffith close, even though he knew he shouldn't want that. He shouldn't allow himself to get close to Griffith, because it would make everything harder than it already was.

He wasn't sure he could, though. No matter what he thought about it, how he felt about it, Griffith was his mate. That meant something, both to Lawrence and his snake. The fact that they couldn't bond with him or be with him didn't change that.

Griffith still wasn't sure where to look first. He still had no idea where he was and what the people were doing there, and while he wanted to ask, he realized it was time for bed — at least for the others. He didn't think he'd be able to sleep. He was so jacked up, his mind too full of what had happened to-night, what he'd learned.

He was only partly surprised that Lawrence had noticed it when Lawrence asked, "Hey, Win? Is it okay with you if I tell Griffith about us?"

Win didn't immediately understand what Lawrence was talking about, or maybe he did. "Us? I'm sorry, Law, but I'm already bonded."

Lawrence's cheeks flushed. He was adorable, but the more Griffith looked at him, the more he could see something else lurking under the blond, cute surface. There was much more to Lawrence than the cherub impression he gave to the world, and for some reason, Griffith couldn't wait to get to it and to find out about it. "You know what I mean," Lawrence groused.

Win's smile didn't vanish, but he looked at Lawrence as if he were trying to find the answer to a question. "Have you made a decision already?" he asked.

Lawrence's cheeks became redder, and Griffith didn't miss the way he quickly looked at him. "No. But he's in this, obviously, since he wants to help and you're going to use him. We might as well tell him who we are and what we do."

"I suppose you'll have to do it sooner or later, so sure. Tell him."

Griffith would have given anything he owned to find out what they were talking about at this point. He didn't ask, though. He waited until Win had said his goodbyes and disappeared up the stairs by the kitchen to finally burst out, "What are you about to tell me?"

Lawrence smiled.

He should do that more often, and not only because he was even cuter when he smiled. Griffith had the impression that Lawrence didn't smile much, though, and he wanted to change that. The why didn't even matter, not at this point. "Why don't we go upstairs? I'll show you to a guest room and you can, I don't know, shower and go to bed."

Griffith crossed his arms over his chest. "Nope. I want to know. You have the authorization to tell me."

Lawrence's smile widened. "I *will* tell you. But not here."

Griffith was all for spending more time alone with Lawrence in a place where people couldn't accidentally or on purpose interrupt them, so he didn't protest more when Lawrence headed toward the stairs. Instead, he followed him, curious to see where he'd spend the night. He'd been trying to understand what this place was since he'd arrived. It was obviously an old warehouse that had been converted into living spaces. That was the only way to have such a big kitchen-living room combo. It looked like a lot of people shared the place, or maybe it was only a few of them who liked having space. Griffith thought the first one was more probable, though.

There was a reason Lawrence of all people had been sent to get him, and a reason that Win, Lawrence's boss, lived here, along with Lawrence, Beck, Roark, and no doubt their mates. How many other people were around? Griffith couldn't tell right now, but from the number of doors he counted when they reached the top of the stairs, it had to be quite a few.

He became sure of that when Lawrence continued up another flight of stairs.

This floor appeared newer, with a faint scent of paint still lingering in the air. There were as many doors as there had been downstairs, and all of them were closed, but Griffith noticed light coming from under one of them, and he could hear music. It wasn't loud, but enough for him to recognize Debussy. "Who likes classical music?" he asked as he followed Lawrence along the hallway.

"That's Payne."

So there *were* other people around. "Is he one of your friends? Or a coworker?"

"Neither of them. I mean, he *is* a friend, but he's also only seventeen."

Griffith blinked. "Is he someone's son?"

"No, but it's not my story to tell, and now isn't the moment. I'm sure you have more pressing questions than how Payne got here. You'll find out anyway if you stick around."

Griffith wanted to stick around. He realized it was ridiculous. He'd just met Lawrence, and Lawrence hadn't given him any hint that he might be interested in more than the information he might be able to get from his father. Griffith *was* interested, though. How could he not? Lawrence was cute, but there was a hidden darkness and depth in his eyes, and the way he'd taken care of Griffith even though he hadn't known that Griffith didn't have anything to do with his father's work had to mean something. He could have thrown Griffith this way and that to get answers, but instead of doing that, he'd untied him and fed him.

And that kiss.

Griffith had managed not to focus on it until now, mostly by reminding himself that it was the way Lawrence had used to knock him out. He was sure of it, even though he couldn't explain how it worked. So Lawrence had kissed him only to put him out of commission, but Griffith couldn't stop thinking about how Lawrence's lips had felt, soft and slightly wet.

"This is your room for the night," Lawrence said, pushing open one of the doors.

The bedroom was more luxurious than Griffith would have thought, since he doubted the warehouse saw a lot of guests. The bed was huge, the furniture was dark wood, and from what he could see of the bathroom, it was big enough to house a small elephant. "Wow. Thank you." Griffith's apartment wasn't this nice, so he was going to enjoy it, even though he suspected he'd be mostly sleeping. He was exhausted, although not enough to forego one last chat with Lawrence.

He put his messenger bag onto the dresser and flopped into the armchair by the window. "So, who are you? And don't tell me Lawrence, because you know that's not what I mean."

Lawrence smiled. "I wasn't going to say that, but okay." He cleared his throat. "First things first, you don't have to fear anyone in this house. We're not going to hurt you."

Griffith cocked his head. This wasn't going the way he'd thought it would. "I know that."

"How can you? You have no idea where you are and what you walked into the middle of."

"Maybe, but I trust you. Like you said earlier, you could have hurt me while I was unconscious, but you didn't. You fed me and made sure I was okay. That's enough for me to trust you."

"I don't know if I should be angry at how trusting you are or relieved that it'll make my job easier," Lawrence muttered. He raked a hand through his hair. "So you know about the council."

"Everyone does." Ever since one of its members had been outed more than a decade earlier.

"And you know about the enforcers."

Griffith resisted the urge to roll his eyes. "I do. Where are you going with that? You're not an enforcer. You don't wear the uniform."

Lawrence smirked. "Not all of them always wear it. But anyway, me and Win, and almost everyone else in the warehouse work for the council. We're not enforcers, though, like you said. We're the council assassins."

That sounded ignominious, so Griffith wasn't surprised that Lawrence had tried to reassure him before telling him. "I suppose that word means exactly what it usually means," he said.

"It does." The smile was gone from Lawrence's face. "All the assassins are people who were experimented on and who left the labs different than they were when they went in. We all have an ability we didn't before. Well, except for Win. He's our handler, the guy in charge."

"Roark?"

"He can manipulate people's minds to make them see what he wants them to see. He could make you believe you were in the jungle right now if he wanted to."

That sounded so fucking interesting, and Griffith was dying to analyze Roark's DNA and see how different it was from a normal shifter's. He didn't say that out loud, though. He had enough experience working with sifters and humans who'd gone through the labs to know how touchy most of them were. They didn't want to feel like experiments again, even though it was to try to help them

"What about you?" he asked instead. "What's your ability?"

Lawrence didn't want to tell Griffith what his ability was. He didn't know how Griffith would react to it, but it would probably be either in awe or else as though Lawrence was a science experiment, and that was the last thing Lawrence needed right now. He didn't care if Griffith wanted to examine him. Or whatever, but not right now. Not tonight. He didn't want to break the feeble connection between them, the possibilities that were there even though he knew better than to believe in them.

"So, this is your room," he said.

Griffith rolled his eyes. "Fine, don't tell me. I have a pretty good idea already anyway." He eyed Lawrence. "So you're an assassin?"

Lawrence crossed his arms over his chest. "I know I don't look like much, but yes."

"Who said you didn't look like much? I'd imagine that your appearance helps when you have to . . . work. I certainly never suspected there was more to you than a sweet little lost man."

Lawrence would have bristled at those words if anyone else had said them. He couldn't bring himself to feel angry, though, not at Griffith. It was already a miracle Griffith wasn't running for the hills screaming bloody murder—or rather, murderers. Because that was what Lawrence and the others were. They killed people—bad people, people who deserved it and who were a danger to society and shifters, but people nonetheless. Lawrence wouldn't be surprised if Griffith was horrified by that and if he never wanted to see him again come morning. He was surprised his mate hadn't already had a strong reaction. "Why are you still here?" he asked. He might not be planning to tell Griffith they were mates, but he was curious. He wanted to get to know Griffith, to find out what made him tick, what he liked and disliked.

Griffith blinked. "What do you mean?"

"I just told you I'm a killer, that most people in this house are, yet you're not trying to leave."

Griffith linked his fingers together and laid his hands on his stomach. He peered at Lawrence until Lawrence wanted to squirm, but he didn't move. He was trained to stay still, after all, even though standing under his mate's gaze was the hardest thing he'd ever done.

"Who do you kill?" Griffith asked.

"People who deserve it."

"Like? Give me an example."

"Like the people who had Payne and a bunch of other kids locked in a dank warehouse. They trafficked the kids to humans, mostly, but also to other shifters. They were used as slaves and pets until their *owner* got tired. Then they exchanged them."

"So you guys killed the traffickers, right? The people who probably kidnapped the kids or bought them, the people who sold them and made a profit of their pain and suffering."

"Yes."

"What would have happened if you'd arrested them?"

"I have no way to know. Most of them were humans, so we'd have had to hand them over to the human justice system."

"And that never goes well. Trust me, I know about how things work. I read enough newspapers. I hate the way shifters are still treated, like their lives matter less than humans.

So yes, I do understand why the council takes things in hand and makes the decisions."

"You're not afraid of me? Of us? You're not horrified by the blood on my hands?" Lawrence knew most people would have nightmares of the killings, would regret what they'd done. He had, in the beginning. The first few times he'd killed someone had made a mess out of him, and he hadn't slept a full night for months after that.

But he was over it. He'd seen too much, had listened to too many tortured, trafficked people to regret taking care of the people who had hurt them. He'd continue to do it because someone needed to. Someone needed to protect shifters, both from other shifters and from humans who saw them as little more than animals they could dispose of any way they wanted.

"No."

Lawrence frowned — Griffith hadn't even hesitated. "Most people would be. Most people would tell us to let human justice or even the enforcers take care of it, as it should be."

"Why don't you? I mean, why don't the enforcers do this? They're the armed hand of the council, right? And you, I guess you're the shadow."

"The enforcers have to respect the rules the government gave the council."

"But you don't."

"No. We do what the council orders. They don't make this kind of decision quickly or easily. You have no idea what's been happening, what we have to do to protect ourselves and the shifters in this country."

"I can guess it has to do with what my father is doing. You had to find out somehow, and I can't imagine it was easy. My father has always been secretive about his work, and now I understand why. He always said it was top secret stuff that he couldn't talk about, and I didn't push. I knew the government wasn't perfect, but I never thought . . ." Griffith sighed. "I feel like I have to apologize for what we're doing to your people."

"You don't." But the fact that he felt this way was one more indication of the kind of man Griffith was, and Lawrence liked what he was finding out about his mate. Leaving him behind was going to be hell, but it was the best thing Lawrence could do for Griffith, so it wasn't even a question that he'd do it. What he wanted or didn't want didn't matter. He was what he was, and there was no changing it. He wouldn't risk poisoning Griffith and putting his life in danger. He'd already done that tonight, and his heart raced just thinking about what could have happened if he'd been distracted, if he'd put a little more venom in his kiss.

"I know that, rationally. But I've met so many people who have been hurt in the labs. I don't work with them, but I do make a point of being there when a new therapy is tried. We've had some results, but nothing groundbreaking yet." He sighed. "I wish I could do more. That's why I want to find out what my father is doing, and if I can, I want to put a stop to it. Too many people have already been hurt, and for what? Money? The ability to win wars? Those things don't make sense to me, especially not when lives are being sacrificed for them."

Griffith was perfect, or perfect for Lawrence anyway. How was Lawrence supposed to walk away from him? He was strong—he'd had to be when he was in the lab, and he hadn't let himself relax since then—but this was something he'd never gone against.

No one was hurting him. No one was experimenting on him. He couldn't fight back with his hands or with his training. He didn't know how to protect himself from Griffith, from letting him carve his way under his skin and into his heart. He wasn't even sure that was possible.

Griffith leaned forward. "So no, I'm not afraid of you. Like you said, some people might be horrified, but I've always thought that justice can't get everywhere and that the people who can't be reached need to be taken care of anyway. They're dangerous, and if it's their life against dozens of lives, then I wouldn't hesitate to kill them myself." He shrugged. "I have no doubt I'd have nightmares after that, but I'd deal with them. Some people don't deserve to live. That's all I'm saying."

This wasn't going the way Lawrence had thought it would. He'd half hoped that Griffith would never want to see him again. It would have made things so much easier for him.

But Griffith wasn't going anywhere, was he? Even if he never came back to the warehouse, Lawrence would know he was out there, that he probably wouldn't say no to being with him. He had to feel the pull of the bond, the need to be as close to Lawrence as Lawrence wanted to be to him. Lawrence hoped he didn't know what it meant, but he had no doubt that Griffith would figure it out if they spent more time together. The man was smart, so much more than Lawrence. He knew what mates were, just like everyone else in the country, hell, in the world.

Lawrence had to stay away, but would he be able to?

Maybe Griffith should have cared more about the kind of job Lawrence did. Maybe he should have left like Lawrence clearly had expected him to when he'd told him about it.

He wasn't going anywhere, though.

He didn't know what it was about Lawrence, but Griffith wanted to know more. He was also fascinated with everything Lawrence had told him. Not surprised—it made sense that the council had a group of people they used to protect themselves, especially in light of what Griffith's father was doing. Griffith was slightly surprised that they killed people, and worried they'd kill his father, but that was it. His mom would be destroyed if something happened to his father, but Griffith was confident she'd get better. He didn't want his father to die, but if it happened, he wouldn't be heartbroken. He could imagine all too well what his father was doing in his lab now that he knew part of it, and he hated it.

"What your father is doing doesn't have anything to do with you," Lawrence suddenly said.

Griffith wasn't even surprised at the fact that Lawrence could read him so well anymore. "I know. I have no control over his actions. That doesn't mean I'm not worried or that I don't feel guilty."

Lawrence hesitated.

Griffith wanted to tell him he could say or ask whatever he wanted, but he didn't. Lawrence was clearly on his guard about something, and until Griffith knew what that something was, he didn't want to push. He didn't want to risk whatever they could have—and he knew they *could* have something. He was sure of it. He *needed* to be sure of it, because he could tell that Lawrence was going to do his best to keep his distance.

"What about your mother?" Lawrence asked.

"What about her?"

"Do you think she knows what your father is doing?"

Oh. He was worried that Griffith might lose both of his parents at the same time. "She doesn't."

"You're sure?"

"Yes. Trust me, my father would never talk about his job to her. She's . . ." Griffith wasn't sure how to explain. He didn't want to talk badly about his mother. He loved her, and she'd raised him as best as she could. He couldn't deny the fact that she was weak, though. It didn't make her a bad mother, or a bad person. "She's been in love with my father forever, but I don't think he ever felt that way toward her. He married her because my grandfather is rich. He wanted the money, probably to finance his experiments, now that I think about it. He didn't get it because my grandfather knew what kind of man he was. He made sure my father will never get a cent of his money."

"I'm sure your father—"

"Nope. I know what you're trying to do, but it's all right. You don't have to. I've always known my father didn't love my mother, or me. We were commodities. I've gotten used to that, so you don't have to comfort me. My mom will be destroyed when he's arrested, or whatever you're planning to do to him eventually, but it'll still be the best thing that will happen to her. She's—he's abusive. He's never hurt her physically, but he doesn't hold back when it comes to telling her in great detail everything she does wrong. She won't leave because she thinks he needs her."

Lawrence rubbed his face. "This is more complicated than I expected."

"You thought you'd use me to get the answers you needed and that you'd then kill my father."

"Pretty much."

"I'm sorry I couldn't do more, but I will." Griffith had no idea what would happen beyond that. He knew better than to think that Lawrence would stick around once he and his boss had what they were looking for, or that he'd be allowed to continue coming here, wherever *here* was. He wasn't one of the council assassins. He wasn't friends or family to any of them, whatever he felt when it came to Lawrence.

"I should leave, let you sleep," Lawrence said. He got up, but Griffith wasn't ready to let him go.

Once he went to sleep, morning would come fast, and he'd have to leave. He didn't know if he'd ever get the chance to be with Lawrence like this again. They weren't doing anything more than talking, but he couldn't forget the kiss they'd shared, even though he knew it hadn't meant the same thing for Lawrence as it did for him.

"You can stay," he said in a rush.

Lawrence frowned. "It's late. You had a hard evening. You *should* sleep."

Griffith sighed. "I don't think I'll be able to. You're right, I *had* a long, hard evening, and I can't stop thinking about what my father is doing. I already know that every time I close my eyes, I'll see the people he's hurting, and I don't think I can stand that. I don't want to find out if I can."

"You can watch TV, I guess. I don't think anyone is going to wake you up early tomorrow morning, don't worry."

Dammit. What was Griffith supposed to say to get Lawrence to stay with him? "Great. We can watch a movie. What were you thinking about?"

"I didn't mean—"

Griffith hoped his expression was as pitiful as he needed it to be. "Please? I don't want to be alone."

He could see how conflicted Lawrence was, and once again, he wondered why. What was going on? Why did Lawrence seem to want to stay as far away as possible from Griffith while at the same time worrying about him?

What the fuck was going on?

Griffith was too tired to think about it. He just wanted to enjoy the rest of the night. He knew he'd fall asleep five minutes into the movie, but he didn't care. "I'm going to go to the bathroom. You pick the movie in the meantime, and when I'm back, we can sit together on the bed and watch it."

He didn't give Lawrence the time to protest. He knew Lawrence would if he was given the opportunity, but he probably would stay otherwise so he wouldn't appear to be rude. Griffith didn't like manipulating people like that, but right now, he couldn't be alone, and Lawrence was the closest thing he had to a friend here. It wasn't like he could call his grandfather and tell him what had happened.

Griffith thought for sure that Lawrence would have left when he finally came out of the bathroom, feeling slightly better after a short shower. He'd had to skip the underwear, so he was wearing only his dress pants, and it wasn't particularly comfortable. All thoughts of comfort fled his mind when he saw Lawrence sitting on the bed, his back against the headboard, the room dark except for the light from the TV. Lawrence had even taken his shoes off, and his feet were small and probably as cute as the rest of him.

Lawrence cleared his throat. "I hope you don't mind. I made myself comfortable."

"Of course not. What did you choose?"

"Die Hard."

"Ah, a classic."

"I thought it would be better to watch something we've probably both already seen. I don't know about you, but I'm tired enough that I might fall asleep in the middle of it."

Griffith hoped that was precisely what would happen. "I agree."

It took them a moment to settle on the bed. Lawrence was tense, his back too straight to be comfortable, and Griffith wasn't quite sure how to behave. He wanted to be closer to Lawrence, but he didn't want to push, so he settled for being close enough to brush against him if he moved, but they weren't touching if they were both still.

And he was right. It took about five minutes for his eyelids to feel heavy. They slid closed on their own, and while he tried to open his eyes a few times, he didn't quite manage. The soft mattress, the stress of the day, and even Lawrence's presence got to him. He felt strangely safe, comforted, and he liked that he was right where he was supposed to be.

That thought made him think of something, but he

couldn't quite grasp it through the fog of exhaustion. He gave up trying and curled into a ball, snuggling close to Lawrence. He knew he probably shouldn't, but he was past caring.

He just wanted to sleep.

CHAPTER FOUR

Lawrence was still thinking about Griffith three days later. He hadn't seen him again, which was both a relief and a pity. He wanted to see Griffith, to make sure he was okay, but he knew it was better that he stay away, like he had the morning after Griffith had spent the night in the warehouse.

They'd fallen asleep together. Griffith had conked out five minutes into the movie, and Lawrence had allowed himself to relax and savor the moment. He would cherish the memories of having Griffith snuggled against his side, softly breathing, safe and sound and so gorgeous that looking at him made Lawrence's heart ache.

He'd left in the morning before Griffith woke up, and he'd made sure to stay in his bedroom until Griffith was gone, taken home by Dasha. Then he'd had to avoid Win's pitying glances. Yes, he hated that he couldn't be with Griffith. He wanted what most of his friends had, but he couldn't have it. Moping over it wouldn't change that fact. Nothing would. Lawrence was the way he was, and there was nothing to do about it. He wasn't going to put Griffith's life in danger just because he didn't want to be alone. *Griffith* was the important one here. He was Lawrence's mate, and Lawrence wanted him to be happy and safe. That second part would only happen if he stayed away, so that was how things were going to be.

"You're moping."

Okay, so maybe it wasn't *that* easy to let go, but did Ulric really have to point it out. "Don't you have something else to do? Maybe somewhere else to be?" Lawrence asked between two breaths. He'd have faked not being able to talk since he was running on the treadmill, but he and Ulric trained together whenever they could, so Ulric would know it was bullshit.

Ulric's eyes narrowed, and he looked more closely at Lawrence. "You really are, aren't you? I thought that maybe you were just, I don't know, tired or something. I was teasing. But there really *is* something going on with you."

Damn it. "Can you just let it go? I want to finish this run and get some weights in before Win finds us something to do." He hoped Win didn't have to be told that he didn't want anything to do with Griffith. As far as he knew, Griffith had been forbidden to ask his father about what he was doing.

Lawrence hadn't been there the morning after Griffith had spent the night, but Win had told him about it. The council had decided that it was too dangerous. They didn't want to put Griffith's life in danger, considering that he was Lawrence's mate as well as the work he did to help humans and shifters. Lawrence wasn't sure that having that kind of order would change anything for Griffith, though. His mate had seemed convinced that the only way to redeem what his father was doing was helping to stop him, even though he had nothing to do with it. Lawrence wanted to go to him and make sure he didn't do anything stupid, but he couldn't.

Ulric stopped his treadmill. "What happened? Law? What's going on?"

Lawrence sighed. He didn't want to talk, even though he knew Ulric was worried because he cared. There was nothing to say, or at least, nothing to say that Lawrence hadn't already thought about and told himself. But this friendship had to go both ways. He'd spent too much time pushing away people after he'd been released from the lab to jeopardize what he had with Ulric.

He slowed his treadmill down enough that he could talk without sounding like he was dying. "I'm okay."

"Sure you are. Now tell me the truth."

"Goddammit, Ulric. Can't you just really be the airhead everyone thinks you are?"

Ulric winked. "Nope. And you better tell me before I call Miles to the rescue."

Miles was their friend, although Lawrence wasn't as close to him as he was to Ulric. Maybe it was because Miles was human, even though he'd been modified, and Lawrence was terrified he'd hurt him. He'd hurt Ulric too if he wasn't careful, but shifters were sturdier.

He jabbed his finger onto the treadmill screen and stopped it. He grabbed his towel and dried his face, knowing full well that wasting time wasn't going to help him get out of this situation.

"Hey, guys," Miles said as he walked into the gym.

Lawrence groaned. Were those two doing it on purpose? Were they cornering him?

"Hey, Miles," Ulric said with a wicked smile. "You're just in time. Lawrence was about to tell me why he's been moping around the past few days."

Miles frowned. "I thought that was obvious."

"Obvious? What do you know that I don't?"

"It's that guy, isn't it? The scientist?"

Lawrence was going to kill them both. "Will you shut up?"

"No, no," Ulric intervened. "I'm interested in this. Tell me more, Miles."

Lawrence knew trying to stop this would be useless. It wasn't like he could forbid them to talk about it when he wasn't there. They were worried, and he understood that. He would be, too, if one of them were in his place.

"I don't know what happened, but yeah, I think it has to do with that guy."

"Griffith," Lawrence supplied. He didn't want his mate to just be that *guy*.

"Yeah, Griffith. Didn't you spend the night with him?"

Ulric's eyes widened. "You did? Lawrence, you sly—"

"Don't finish that," Lawrence growled. "Nothing happened between Griffith and me. We both fell asleep. That's all."

"There had to be more than that, because now that I think about it, Miles is right. You *have* been like this since the day he left." Ulric hesitated. "You know you can talk to us, right? We're not going to make fun of you or tease you if it's serious. Or even if it's not. I swear."

Ulric teased just about anyone on anything, but he was coming from a good place right now, and Lawrence believed him. Or at least, he believed Ulric would *try* not to tease. Sometimes, though, it was as if the impulse was stronger than his willpower. That wasn't going to stop him from telling them what was happening. They were his best friends, and they were worried. No matter how much Lawrence hated making himself vulnerable, if there were two people he trusted with his life, it was Ulric and Miles.

He dropped onto one of the benches that ran along the walls of the gym. "Miles is right. My mood has to do with Griffith."

"Is it because he left? Did you try asking him to stay?" Ulric asked.

Miles elbowed him in the ribs. "Shut up and let the man talk, yeah? That'll be faster than asking him whatever question pops into your mind."

Lawrence agreed, but it made him smile. Ulric's eagerness and affection were what he needed to get over this. He'd be stronger if his friends were behind him than if he were alone. "Griffith is my mate," he said. He didn't know how else to say it, and the sooner the words got out of his mouth, the easier things would be.

Both Ulric and Miles stared. Lawrence had expected a lot of questions, but he got none until Miles blinked and asked, "Why did you let him leave? Why aren't you with him right now?"

"You know what I can do. What I *might* do to him if I'm not careful. I can't risk it."

"You've never hurt any of us," Ulric pointed out.

"I've also never made out with any of you."

Ulric grimaced. "Good point. What did Griffith say?"

"He doesn't know."

Miles sighed. "Oh, Lawrence. Why haven't you told him?"

"Because I didn't see the point. I might not know him well, but I doubt he'd have left as easily as he did if he'd known."

"Of course he wouldn't have. He's your mate. Even though he doesn't know, I'm ready to bet he's thinking about you. He's as drawn to you as you are to him. The only difference is that he's probably confused, because he doesn't understand why or what's going on."

That wasn't exactly true — Griffith was human after all, so things were different for him — but Lawrence knew that Miles was at least in part right. Griffith was probably wondering what was happening to him, and he wouldn't find out until Lawrence told him.

But Lawrence wouldn't. He *couldn't*. Right?

Griffith was going crazy. He had to be. That was the only explanation he had for the fact that he couldn't seem to stop thinking about Lawrence.

He'd met the man once. He'd fallen asleep against him. That was all there was to it. Lawrence certainly hadn't seemed to have a problem forgetting about Griffith. He hadn't been in the room when Griffith had woken up, and Griffith hadn't seen him again. He didn't know if Lawrence had been avoiding him or if he'd just been busy, but did it matter? Lawrence knew where to find him if he wanted to. He'd known where to find him when he'd come to kidnap him.

What was worse was that after thinking he could help, Griffith had been told to stay put. He understood it, in a way—he was just a guy the council didn't know if they could trust, and it was his father who was doing all those terrible things. He still wanted to help, though. He *needed* to do it.

That was why he was standing in front of his parents' house right now. When his mother had called him yesterday to once again ask him to come for dinner, he'd said yes. He could tell his mom had been surprised. She probably only called because she felt she had to. They both knew how uncomfortable dinner was going to be, but this was necessary. He needed the answers, and more importantly, the council needed them.

Griffith knew what it would mean for his father eventually. Once the council had everything they needed, they'd probably bring charges to the government. They couldn't exactly make Griffith's father disappear, not when he worked for the government. So he'd be arrested. If he wasn't, if the government tried to hide him or whatever, then they'd make sure Griffith's father wouldn't be able to hurt anyone ever again. Griffith wasn't sure how he felt about that—he didn't want anyone to die, but he'd never loved his father, and he did think the man had to pay.

But he couldn't think about that now.

He raised his hand and knocked on the door.

He heard his mother's heels clicking on the hallway tiles as she walked to the door. It had been a while since he'd last seen her, but she still looked the same—hair perfectly coiffed, a row of pearls at her neck, clothes neat. Her smile was brittle, though, as if she knew that Griffith was there to make trouble.

"Griffith."

Griffith forced himself to smile. He knew she was going to be hurt when everything went down and that she might not want to see him again when she realized the part he'd had in this, but it needed to be done. She'd forgive him, in time, and if she didn't, well, Griffith would have done what he thought was right. It would hurt, but it would be worse if he knew about this but didn't do anything to fix it. "Hey, Mom."

She stepped aside to let him in. He kissed her cheek, inhaling the scent so familiar to him. He'd missed her, and he hadn't even realized how much. He hoped he'd still have the chance to see her once everything was said and done, and maybe to heal their relationship.

His father destroyed everything he touched, didn't he?

"Your father is in the dining room," she murmured as she stepped away.

Of course he was. He was waiting for her to serve him dinner, just like he had every night of Griffith's childhood. Some things never changed. "I'll help you in the kitchen."

She looked horrified at that suggestion. "Oh, no. You know what he'd think of that. Go and sit down. Dinner will be served in ten minutes."

Griffith sighed, but he obeyed. His mom was obviously nervous, and he didn't want to make it worse. "All right. Thank you, Mom."

Griffith didn't want to do this. He didn't want to see his father. But he was going to.

It took a lot for him to walk into the dining room. His father was sitting at the head of the table reading files. He put them away when he saw Griffith standing there, but he limited himself to putting them onto the cabinet by the wall. "Griffith. Your mother told me you were coming, but I didn't think you actually would."

Griffith swallowed. He needed to get this right on his first try. "I should have come sooner," he said as he slid into his chair. "But I've been working a lot. Too much, probably. Hoffman is working me to the bones."

His father frowned. "Hard work has never scared you."

"It still doesn't. There's a difference between hard work that's rewarded and hard work that isn't."

"Is Hoffman not paying you enough?"

"I suppose some might think he is, but *I* think I deserve more." Griffith smiled and hoped it wasn't a grimace. "But enough about me. What are *you* working on? I've always been curious, and while I know you can't tell me everything, now that we're in the same field, I wouldn't mind hearing at least some of it."

"Ah, well. You know what I'm working on is top secret."

"I do. I'm your son, though, and I promise I won't say anything. Who would I talk to, anyway? It's not like I have friends who can understand what it's about."

His father's eyes narrowed, but to Griffith's surprise, he didn't call him on the bullshit he was spewing. "I work with shifters."

"Oh? Well, it's similar to what I'm doing, then."

"It's not. You want to take away what makes them special. I don't."

Griffith gritted his teeth. "I want to help them go back to what they were before people hurt them without their consent. That's entirely different."

"Is it?"

Griffith's father leaned forward, but his mother walked into the room just as he opened his mouth, and he closed it, leaning back as she served him dinner.

Griffith tried to ask more questions as they ate. His mother was silent—she always seemed to be—but his father wasn't answering. He always found a way to walk the discussion back to Griffith's work rather than his own, and Griffith was getting nervous.

"I'll go get dessert," Griffith's mother murmured, getting up and grabbing her plate.

Griffith knew better than to ask her if he could help. He stayed where he was, waiting, hoping that maybe once she was gone his father would finally talk.

"What are you playing at?" his father snapped as soon as the dining room door closed behind his wife.

"Playing at? Nothing."

"Why are you asking all those questions about my job, then?"

This was it. The moment that could break or make this. "I'm just curious. I told you I'm not happy where I am anymore. I was just wondering if maybe I had a shot at coming to work with you." Griffith slid his phone out of his pocket as he talked. He didn't like the way this conversation was going, and he wanted to be sure someone knew what he was doing. He should have done that *before* starting it, but he hadn't thought his father would hurt him.

He wasn't so sure of that now.

His father had never touched him, not in anger, not in love, but the gleam in his eyes made Griffith uneasy.

"Working with me? Did you think I'd believe that? You're a bleeding heart. You've always been."

"I don't see what that has to do with the job." Luckily for Griffith, Win had given him his number before he'd left the warehouse. It was easy to send an SOS to him and put his phone away, all while barely glancing at his lap.

"You don't want to hurt them."

Griffith knew what his father was talking about, but he faked ignorance. He was pretty sure the best thing for him right now would be wasting time until someone could come to help him. "Hurt them? What are you talking about?"

"I work for the government. You know that. Do you think

they want us to *help* shifters?"

Of course Griffith didn't. He should have realized that a while ago. He'd buried his head in the sand, but that was over now. He was going to have to face his father and what he did, and that was okay.

Hopefully, he wouldn't be alone doing it, though. He needed help. He knew he did.

"Law."

Lawrence blinked up at Win. "Yes?" He was still trying to digest the dinner Graham had put together—roast, potatoes, carrots, homemade bread. Lawrence had eaten too much, and he was feeling it.

"Griffith needs help."

That got Lawrence right out of his food coma. He sprang up, pushing Ulric's legs off his lap. "What? What happened? Where is he?"

"Come with me."

Lawrence wanted to rush Win as they went to his office, but Win was going as fast as he could. Besides, if Griffith was about to be hurt, Win would have sent the first person who could have taken care of it. He wouldn't have come back to the kitchen to get Lawrence.

"What happened?" Lawrence asked again as soon as they were in Win's office. Beck was there, typing away on his computer. He didn't even look up, but Lawrence didn't care.

"He texted me an SOS. I had Beck track him through his phone. He's at his parents' house."

"I thought you told him to stay away from his father?"

"I told him the council had decided he shouldn't try to find out more about what his father is doing. The man is still his father, though. We can't exactly force him to stay away from him."

"You know he went there to get answers." If there was one thing Lawrence was sure of, it was that.

"That's what I suspect, yes. He was keen on helping, on trying to redeem himself."

"He doesn't need to redeem himself. He hasn't done anything. And what's going on? Why is he sending you an SOS from his father's house?" He'd probably tried to get the answers and hadn't been discreet about it. His father would have realized what was going on, at least in part. What was he going to do? Would he go as far as hurting his only son?

"We don't know, but Dasha is going to shimmer you there. Update us when you can. I'll have everyone on standby, just in case." Win squeezed Lawrence's shoulder. "Go to him and make sure he's safe."

He didn't have to say it twice. It didn't look like anyone knew what was going on, so Lawrence was going to have to go in blind.

It wouldn't be the first time, and it wouldn't be the last.

Dasha was waiting in the hallway. He didn't say anything, just grabbed Lawrence's hand. Lawrence was lucky Win had thought about grabbing weapons on their way to his office.

"Damn it."

Lawrence looked around. They were in a backyard. The lights in the house in front of them were on, and from where they were, Lawrence could see Griffith.

He was sitting at a table with an older man who had to be his father. He didn't quite look like the picture Win had of him, but then, having a black heart would make you look older and uglier.

"The house is shielded," Dasha said.

Of course it was. "Go back and grab a few people, just in case. I'm going in."

"Human or snake?"

"Probably snake. I'll be able to get to Griffith without

anyone noticing me and make sure he actually needs my help before I barge in." Lawrence noticed an empty pot by the back door. It wasn't right next to it, and there was a bag of earth and a few smaller pots of flowers by it as if someone had been planning on putting them into the bigger pot but hadn't yet gotten to it. "I'll hide my stuff in there," he said, tilting his chin toward the pot.

"I'll be back as soon as possible, but we'll hang out here until you let us know or something happens."

Lawrence nodded without looking away from the window. Griffith looked uncomfortable, but as far as Lawrence could see, he wasn't afraid, and his father wasn't about to hurt him.

He slunk toward the back door. A woman was in the kitchen, probably Griffith's mother. She was putting together three plates with her lips pinched together.

Lawrence eyed the door as he undressed. He could probably find a way to get in once he was shifted, but the easiest way would be to have someone open the door for him.

Once he was naked and his clothes were safe, he pressed himself against the wall right next to the door, quickly knocked, and shifted.

There was a pause in the kitchen, the hesitant footsteps. "Who is it?" Griffith's mother asked. Lawrence couldn't see her from where he was. He needed to make sure *she* wouldn't notice him, because she'd no doubt start screaming if she did. People tended to do that when they saw snakes mere inches away from them.

The door opened. "Who is it?" Griffith's mother asked again. She took a step outside and looked around, and Lawrence knew he wouldn't get a better chance. He slithered behind her and hurried into the house.

He could move quickly even as a snake, although it did take him a bit longer to get to places. He went to hide by the open kitchen door. He had a vague idea of where the dining room was, but he'd noticed that the doors there were closed, and he didn't have hands to open them. He was going to have to follow Griffith's mother when she went back and pray that Griffith's father wouldn't hurt him in the meantime.

Griffith's mother came back in and closed the door. Hopefully, she thought she'd imagined the knock, and she wouldn't mention it.

She went back to work on the plates while Lawrence waited. He wanted to go to Griffith, but he knew Griffith wouldn't appreciate it if he barged in while he was getting the answers they needed. That didn't mean Lawrence wasn't going to bust his ass as soon as they were safe, though. There was a reason the council had changed their mind about having Griffith asking questions. No one knew how White might react, and having his son ask the questions might make things better — or worse.

Griffith's mother finally took two of the plates and left the kitchen. She left the door open, and Lawrence went after her. She'd have to go back for the last plate, so he should be able to sneak into the dining room.

There he was. He went to the left, where a heavy-looking piece of furniture stood. There was enough space under it for Lawrence to hide for a moment and check his surroundings.

"I don't know what you're playing at," Griffith's father said. "But you need to stop."

"I'm not playing at anything. You're right when you say I didn't know much about your job, but I'd sign whatever you had to sign."

Griffith's father shook his head and leaned back when his wife placed a plate in front of him. She walked to Griffith and did the same, then left.

"You're not going to get anything from me, Griffith," Gavin White snapped. He was focused on his son's face, and

Lawrence hoped it would be enough for him to get to Griffith.

He slithered along the designs of the thick carpet, hoping they would help disguise his body. He was relieved when he got under Griffith's chair just as his mother walked back in.

Lawrence hesitated. He wanted Griffith to know someone had come to help, but he didn't want to break the conversation yet. He didn't know if Griffith had gotten anything from his father, but he still might, and that wouldn't happen if Lawrence barged into the conversation.

He needed to take a risk.

He moved closer to Griffith's leg and poked his head under the hem of Griffith's pants. He felt Griffith go tense, but when he didn't say anything about the snake trying to get into his pants, Lawrence guessed he wouldn't and that he'd realized what was happening.

He moved upward, wrapping his body around Griffith's leg, squeezing gently. He settled himself halfway up Griffith's tibia and brushed the tip of his tail against Griffith's skin in what he hoped was a reassuring gesture rather than one that would freak Griffith out.

Griffith hadn't reacted except when he'd jerked as Lawrence slithered up his leg. He'd managed not to say anything, though, so Lawrence was pretty sure no one else knew he was there. The conversation that was going on above his head was normal enough—it seemed that Griffith and his father didn't want to continue their conversation with Griffith's mother present.

Now Lawrence had to wait.

Griffith had almost screamed when he'd felt something touch his leg. He'd looked down and had found himself face to face with a snake.

A *fucking* snake.

He had no idea what kind of snake it was, if it was harmless or if it was venomous. He suspected it was Lawrence, or another shifter Win had sent, but he couldn't be sure. He supposed that the fact that the snake hadn't bit him yet was a clue to that, but maybe it was just biding its time. Maybe it was going to bite, and Griffith would drop dead in his plate of mille-feuille dessert that his mother had baked.

He tried to focus on his plate instead of the snake — or his father. He wasn't sure which one would be worse at this point.

"It was delicious, Mom," he told his mother when she got up to take away the empty plates. He'd had enough of waiting and hiding. Lawrence was there, so he'd be safe even if he did confront his father, or at least he hoped so. Trying to be inconspicuous hadn't worked, and Griffith didn't think it would. His father knew something was up, so he might as well just come out with it and see what happened.

The door swung shut behind his mother, and Griffith attacked. "I know what you're doing," he told his father.

He wasn't surprised when his father's only reaction was to arch a brow. "Oh?"

"At your lab. You're experimenting on shifters."

His father leaned back in his chair. "So that's why you came today. Who sent you? Your boss? He should have known better. You're a terrible actor."

Griffith had known he was, but there wasn't much he could do about it. He also didn't want his father to know that he was working for the council right now. "You can't keep on hurting those people," he said instead of answering.

"They're not people, Griffith. I thought I'd taught you that."

"You certainly tried. But whatever they can shift into, they're as human as me and probably more so than you."

Griffith's father slammed his palm on the table. "Don't talk to me like that, Griffith. I'm still your father."

God, how much Griffith wanted to tell him he wasn't, not anymore. He couldn't hurt his mother, though, not right now. Not when he knew something worse was coming for his father. "Why? Why are you doing it?"

"Why do you think? Because I *can* do it. Because I'm paid to do it. Because they're only animals. They don't deserve anything different. Their pain will make us better, stronger."

Griffith pushed his chair away and got up. He hoped the snake around his leg was holding on tightly, because there was no way he was staying there a second longer. "You're a monster."

"You got the wrong man, Griffith. I'm human. *They* are monsters."

Griffith wasn't entirely sure he wouldn't throw up his dinner into his mother's rose bushes, so he rushed out of the house and to his car. He ignored his mom's calls, knowing his father would come up with an excuse for his behavior. She'd accept it because that was what she always did.

Griffith stopped at the driver's door and put his hands onto the car roof. He closed his eyes and breathed in and out until the nausea was gone. He wasn't sure how he managed, but he did, and once he didn't feel like puking his guts anymore, he slid into his seat and closed the door.

"Okay, I really hope you're a shifter," he murmured as he raised the leg of his pants and peered at the snake wound around his leg.

The snake peered back. There was intelligence in its gaze, but Griffith was still relieved when the snake slowly nodded.

He swallowed. "Right. Okay. I'm going to take you off my leg and put you into the passenger seat, okay? I'll throw my jacket on top of you so you can shift without flashing me." Although if this snake was Lawrence, Griffith wouldn't mind getting flashed. He doubted Lawrence was of the same opinion, though.

Griffith reached for the snake, but he couldn't bring himself to touch it. What did a snake feel like? Would it be cold or warm? Slimy? "Sorry. I'm not afraid or anything," he tried to explain. "Okay, that's a lie. I'm freaking out because I have no idea who you are. But that's not why I'm not touching you. I've never touched a snake, that's all. And I know you're not a snake. You're a person."

He gently touched the snake's head with a fingertip. The snake closed its little eyes, looking almost like a puppy. It was different shades of brown, with a diamond-like pattern on its back. Griffith relaxed. This wasn't a dangerous animal. This was a shifter, and whoever it was, he or she wouldn't hurt Griffith. He was sure of it.

Or he had to believe it, anyway.

The snake's skin was smooth and warm, not at all like Griffith had imagined. He gently unwound it from his leg and put it down in the passenger seat, even though he wanted to continue stroking it. Then he shrugged off his jacket and gently laid it on top of the snake.

He wasn't surprised when a blond head appeared. He'd suspected this was Lawrence. It made sense that it was him, didn't it? Griffith wasn't sure why, but he knew it did.

"What the fuck were you thinking?" Lawrence snapped.

Griffith hadn't expected this anger. "I was trying to help."

"*Trying* being the word. You didn't get anything from him. He realized what was happening right away. You put yourself in danger for nothing, Griffith."

"I wasn't in danger."

"Of course you were. That man experiments on shifters, and probably humans, for the government. Do you really think he wouldn't have done anything if you'd kept on pushing the way you were?"

Griffith opened his mouth to say that yes, he did believe

that, but he stopped before letting the words out. *Was* he sure? Yes, it was his father he'd been talking to, but he didn't know the man who'd helped bring him into the world. He never had, and what he'd learned from the council highlighted that fact.

He sighed and rubbed his forehead. "I need to start the car before my father starts suspecting something is up. Should I take you somewhere?" He wasn't sure where the warehouse was—it made sense since the assassins were a super-secret group and whatnot—but it might be in town for all he knew.

"I'm coming home with you. I need your phone."

Griffith wasn't going to protest. Lawrence was coming home with him, and he was still naked. That meant that either he'd stay naked—and Griffith was ready to admit that this was his preferred scenario of what would happen—or Griffith would have to lend him some clothes. Or maybe Lawrence was about to call his Nix friend and have him come pick him up at Griffith's place, but that wasn't a scenario Griffith was ready to think about right now.

He handed his phone off to Lawrence and started the car. He tried to focus on the road, but it was impossible for him not to hear Lawrence's side of the conversation.

"Win? Yes, he's safe." Pause. "No, not as far as I know, although I'll make sure to ask him when we get to his place. Can you tell Dasha to pick up my clothes? He knows where I left them." Pause. "I think I will, yes. You know how it is."

How what was? Griffith would have given anything to know what Lawrence was talking about. He *needed* to know. He needed to know everything he could about this man, and he had no idea why. That fact drove him crazy. He'd become a scientist because he wanted to help people, but also because he liked to know how things worked, why they were the way they were. In his case, he found out what genetic mutations did, and hopefully, he managed to reverse it.

In Lawrence's case, though, Griffith had no idea why he was so drawn to the man.

"Don't worry about me. I'll be fine," Lawrence told Win. Griffith thought Win might need to worry about his sanity if Lawrence stayed with him for the night, but he didn't think this was the right moment to say something like that.

Since Lawrence was distracted, Griffith took a moment to look at him. He couldn't stare since he was driving, and the sky was dark, but the streetlamps they passed under were enough for him to see the acres of pale skin, the surprisingly well-defined chest, and the powerful-looking shoulders. Lawrence might be small, but that didn't make him weak.

If anything, it made him fucking hot, and Griffith wasn't sure what he was going to do if Lawrence spent the night in his apartment.

Humiliate himself, probably.

CHAPTER FIVE

Lawrence had to keep his lips pressed together not to yell. He didn't want to freak Griffith out—although he suspected he'd already done so—but fuck, he'd been terrified.

What had Griffith been thinking? He'd faced one of the evilest men around and had asked him questions about what he did in his secret laboratory as if it were a normal thing. The fact that White was his father didn't mean the man was going to give him a pass, for fuck's sake, and Lawrence wished Griffith could see that. He didn't want him to throw himself into danger like he'd done tonight ever again, and he knew how eager Griffith was to help and find answers, but there was a reason Win had told him to back off. Even the council knew it was too dangerous for Griffith—or anyone else right now—to ask those questions.

Lawrence hung up with Win and put the phone down. Win had told him to take the night, thank God. Lawrence was still freaked out over what he'd walked in on, or rather, what he'd slithered in on. He might not be planning to tell Griffith they were mates, but that didn't mean he didn't feel the pull of the bond and the need to protect Griffith with his life if it was necessary. He wanted to lock the man up and make sure he never put himself in such a situation again, but he knew better. Griffith wouldn't accept it, as was right. He was old enough to make his own decisions, no matter how bad they were and how much Lawrence hated them.

"I'm sorry," Griffith muttered.

"What for?" Lawrence didn't like the snappy edge in his

voice, but it was going to take a little while to get it to fade. Fear still rode him and made him want to go back and slam White to the wall for threatening his own son.

Griffith winced. "For making you angry. I understand why you are, but I don't regret what I did."

"Of course you don't."

"I do regret not getting the answers you guys needed."

"You have to stay out of this." He should never have been involved to begin with, but Lawrence wasn't the one who made the decisions when it came to his job, He followed orders, and that was it.

"I don't see how I could help at this point, so I will. But if I *do* think I can find out what you need, then I won't hesitate. I'm sorry, but this needs to be done."

Lawrence pinched the bridge of his nose. He wasn't going to snap again. Griffith didn't deserve it, plus he was afraid of speaking. Lawrence couldn't even explain why he was so panicky, for fuck's sake. That was probably why Griffith was so weirded out. He didn't understand why Lawrence was reacting the way he was, and Lawrence didn't blame him.

He was relieved when they got to Griffith's building and he had to shift again to be carried upstairs. That way, he wasn't risking anything escaping his mouth without him meaning to say it. The need of his snake to tell Griffith they were mates had heightened, probably because of the danger Griffith had been in. The snake didn't understand why they couldn't tell Griffith they were mates. They didn't *have* to bond or to do anything else, but maybe Griffith would be more careful if he knew what he meant to them.

Fat chance of that. Griffith had already made it clear that he'd do what he thought was right, even if it put him in danger.

"You know, I always thought snakes were cold," Griffith murmured when they were in the elevator. Lawrence would have rolled his eyes, but it didn't seem the case. A lot of people thought snakes were cold—and scary. Lawrence didn't usually care, but he had to admit he felt good. It was nice to be cradled against his mate's chest. Griffith was warm, and he smelled good—of laundry detergent and himself, of *mate*.

Lawrence was only partly glad when Griffith locked his apartment door behind them and gently put him on the floor. "I'm going to go grab you some clothes. They'll be big on you, but it's better than being buck ass naked. Unless you want to call Dasha to come to pick you up now that you know I'm safe? You can take my phone again."

Lawrence knew it would be better for both of them if he left. Staying would only make him want more than he could have with Griffith, and he'd risk having Griffith realize what they were. He couldn't bring himself to go, though, not after he felt he'd almost lost Griffith. It wasn't rational, but it didn't make a difference, not right now.

Griffith came back holding folded clothes. Lawrence wasn't sure he wanted to shift, because he suspected Griffith would want to talk if he did. But he itched to touch his mate, to wrap him in his arms and reassure both himself and his snake their mate was okay.

"I'd like you to stay," Griffith murmured just as Lawrence shifted.

Lawrence almost laughed when Griffith slammed his eyes shut and blindly handed him the clothes. He'd noticed that Griffith had been looking at him in the car, but it would be more obvious here, since Lawrence wasn't on the phone. Lawrence didn't mind—thinking that his mate liked his body made him want to puff up his chest in pride—but again, he couldn't exactly say that. It felt good to know that Griffith didn't just see the scrawny, short man most people saw, although that might be because he'd seen Lawrence naked. Still, the result was the same. Griffith liked Lawrence's body, or at least Lawrence thought he did.

He quickly put on the clothes Griffith was still holding at arm's length. They were too big, but they smelled of Griffith, and Lawrence never wanted to change. He'd keep the clothes if he could get away with it.

"Lawrence? Will you stay?"

Lawrence cleared his throat. "I already told Win I would."

Griffith nodded, and Lawrence thought that was the end of that until he asked, "Why?"

"Why what?"

"Why are you staying? You know I'm safe. I don't have information to give you."

"Your father could be on the phone with his boss right now telling him you know what's going on in that lab of his. The council can't risk your life."

Griffith's expression fell. "Oh."

Dammit. Lawrence had suspected Griffith was asking for a reason, and he was sure of it now. He couldn't tell his mate the truth, though. Knowing what he did of Griffith—and that was entirely too much, since Lawrence had been researching his mate's social media accounts because he couldn't stop thinking about him—he suspected Griffith liked him and wanted him to *want* to stay. And Lawrence did. He just couldn't admit it.

"I should probably check what I have in the fridge for dinner."

"I can make do with a pizza," Lawrence told him. He wanted the smile to come back on Griffith's lips, but he didn't know how to do it.

"I've seen how you eat, remember? I can't cook anything close to that, but I can try."

Lawrence caught Griffith's arm and stopped him before he could hide in the kitchen, which had no doubt been his objective. "You don't have to try. Graham's a professional cook, and he gets paid to feed us the way he does. I don't expect you to cook for me." Lawrence didn't want Griffith to cook because it would take away from the short time they had together. He wasn't sure they'd ever have an occasion like this one again, and while spending the night alone with Griffith terrified him, Lawrence wasn't about to back out.

Griffith turned to face Lawrence. He cocked his head as if he were trying to read Lawrence, and Lawrence dropped his hand. He cleared his throat again. "What I mean is that pizza is good and that I'll be happy about it. Graham always insists on making it when we want it, but he makes a healthy one, and while it's good, I want oil and fat and everything else."

"You want to be naughty."

Lawrence knew his cheeks were flaming. "That's not what I said. Graham isn't my father. The only reason he decides what I eat is that he's the one cooking."

"What are you doing here, Lawrence? Are you staying only to make sure my father doesn't come to kill me in my sleep? Or is there something else?"

Just the thought of Griffith being hurt made Lawrence queasy. "You need to be protected. You wouldn't be in this position if the council hadn't sent me to kidnap you."

"So you feel it's your duty to protect me. That's why you're here."

Lawrence wanted to say yes, but he didn't want to lie to his mate.

He wasn't sure he had a choice, though.

Griffith *knew* there was more to it. He was sure of it, and he wanted Lawrence to admit it.

"It's my job," Lawrence said without looking at Griffith.

Griffith gritted his teeth. God, this man was frustrating. But Griffith had taken a moment to think about things, and to face something he'd been avoiding thinking about since he and Lawrence had met. He didn't want to wonder why a shifter was denying their mate the knowledge of what they were. He didn't want to wonder why Lawrence hadn't told him if that was what was happening. Maybe he didn't like Griffith. Maybe he didn't think Griffith was good enough.

Well, fuck him. "Am I your mate?" Griffith asked. He was done walking on eggshells around Lawrence, even though they'd been together only twice counting tonight. He wanted answers, and if Lawrence wasn't going to give them to him, he could leave.

Not that Griffith was going to tell Lawrence that.

Several emotions played on Lawrence's face. Griffith didn't try to identify them because he didn't want to make himself hope, but he recognized the shock, probably that Griffith had understood what was happening on his own. It hadn't been hard once he'd allowed himself to think about it, though. He'd never felt as drawn to anyone as he was to Lawrence, and considering he barely knew Lawrence and that Lawrence was a shifter, there was only one explanation that made sense.

Lawrence sighed. "Yes. You are. How did you know?"

Some of the tension in Griffith's chest loosened. "It makes sense."

"Does it?"

Griffith didn't know why Lawrence wasn't happier about this, but he wasn't going to let it stop him. They were mates, and now that he was sure of it, he was going to do whatever it took for Lawrence to accept that and accept Griffith in his life. Griffith had to find out why Lawrence wasn't happier about it, though. "Why didn't you tell me?"

Lawrence shook his head. "Because it doesn't change anything."

"You're going to have to be more specific. Even if you don't want me because you think I'm an idiot or whatever, I deserve to know."

"I don't think that. I could never think that. But you're right. You deserve to know. Why don't you order dinner? We can talk while we're waiting for it to arrive." Lawrence looked like there was nothing he wanted less than to talk about this, but Griffith wasn't going to miss this opportunity to get answers.

He sat on the couch and placed his order from his phone. He loved that he could use the app rather than call and have the person who answered write down the wrong pizza or whatever. "So? Why?" he asked.

Lawrence blinked. "I thought I'd have a bit more time to think about this."

"There's nothing to think about. I just want to know why you didn't tell me. You can ask me to fuck off once you're done explaining. I'm not going to argue with you if it's something that can't be argued. But I deserve to know." The fact that Lawrence probably would never have told Griffith hurt, but Griffith was still holding onto the possibility that Lawrence had a good reason for keeping him at arm's length.

Lawrence paced the short length of the living, avoiding looking at Griffith.

That was okay with Griffith. He wasn't going to force Lawrence to do anything, and if he was more comfortable not looking at him, then so be it.

"You know I was in a lab," Lawrence finally said.

"Like all the other assassins."

"Yes. That's why we were chosen. We have abilities no one else has. We were trained to use them, and some, like Roark or North, can turn them off and on at will."

"But you can't." Griffith had suspected it when Lawrence had managed to knock him off his feet with only a kiss. No matter how great Lawrence was, there was no way it was normal.

"I can't. I'm a snake shifter. A rattlesnake."

Griffith shivered. If Lawrence had been only a snake, Griffith would probably be, if not dead, not far from it right now. He didn't know much about rattlesnakes, but he did know they could be lethal, especially if one didn't have immediate access to antivenom. "You're venomous."

"I am. I secrete the venom in my bodily fluids, especially saliva. There's less of it in my blood, but it's there."

"That's how you knocked me out?"

"Yes. It took me years to perfect that. I can control how much venom I secrete, although I can't stop secreting it. I use it to knock people out and to kill them. People don't usually suspect me to be anything but a cute little blond, and they let me come close, just like you did."

Griffith's mind was crowded with questions. He knew how snake venom worked, although not in detail — someone was bitten, it entered the bloodstream, and then started to affect the entire body. He had no idea how Lawrence managed to kill someone by kissing them, and he wasn't sure he wanted to find out. He'd have been all over it if anyone but Lawrence had this ability, but he didn't want Lawrence to think he was treating him like a lab rat.

"This is why we can't be together," Lawrence said.

Griffith blinked. What Lawrence was saying did make sense, up to a point. "Why not? I mean, I get that you're not going to want to kiss me since you'd probably knock me out again. That doesn't mean we can't be a couple, though."

Lawrence frowned. "It's not only kissing. I can't have sex with you, or with anyone else. I can't risk it."

"Condoms. Unless there's venom in your sweat, too?" Maybe they could have sex outside so that Lawrence didn't sweat.

Lawrence stopped in front of Griffith. "You're not listening to me. I'm *dangerous*. That's why I'm a council assassin. I can't be close to people."

"You live with the other assassins and their mates, some of which are humans."

"None of them is *my* mate, though. I don't want to climb any of them like a tree."

Griffith blinked. "But you want to climb *me*?" He wasn't used to that. He knew he was decent looking, maybe even cute to some people, but he spent most of his time working, and men didn't often notice him. He had no idea how to flirt or make a guy notice him, and he hadn't cared until now. Knowing that Lawrence wanted to have sex with him made him feel odd. Not proud of his body—he doubted that would ever happen—but like he was more than the geeky scientist people usually saw when they looked at him.

Lawrence rolled his eyes. "Of course I want you. I've wanted you since the first time I saw you in the parking garage."

"That's going to be a nice story to tell our grandkids."

Lawrence closed his eyes. He looked like he was in pain, and Griffith hated his running mouth. Lawrence was trying to tell him something, to explain why they couldn't be together, but Griffith wasn't listening, and he certainly wasn't understanding.

Griffith swallowed. "I understand how hard this might be for you. You're afraid of hurting me. But you said yourself that you can control the amount of venom in your saliva. That means that even if we did make out, you'd probably only knock me out again." Griffith raised a hand before Lawrence could say anything along the line that he didn't want to risk it. "I know. It's just a thought. But, Lawrence, relationships aren't just sex. We can be together even if we never kiss or have sex."

Now Lawrence was looking at Griffith as if he were crazy.

"That wouldn't be fair."

"To whom? Look, I'm going to be honest here. I like sex just fine, but I'm not crazy about it. I can do without, just like I have been since my last boyfriend a few years ago. I *do* want you, but I can make do without sex." That didn't mean he wasn't going to work on Lawrence and find a way for them to do some stuff. Condoms weren't necessary when having sex with shifters, but they were going to become Griffith's best friends apparently, and that was more than okay with him. He was used to condoms. His boyfriends had always been humans, so they'd been necessary.

"What about kissing?" Lawrence asked.

"Okay, I love kissing. But again, I can do without. We can have a relationship that's not physical, and you wouldn't hurt me if we held hands or cuddled."

Lawrence's eyes narrowed. "What about bonding, then? You know I'd have to bite you, and that you'd have to drink my blood for it to happen. That's not possible, not for me. Do you think I'm ready to watch you get old on your own? Actually, scratch that, because I am. But do you think it's fair to you to ask you to stay by my side while you age and I don't? Wouldn't you rather be with someone you can grow with? Someone who will age with you?"

Dammit. Griffith hadn't thought of that yet.

Lawrence could tell Griffith hadn't thought that far yet by the look on his face. He suspected Griffith's mind had been stuck on the romantic side of bonding—spending time together, falling in love. He hadn't yet thought about bonding, because what human thought about marriage the second time they met someone?

"I can find a way," Griffith finally said.

That wasn't the answer Lawrence had expected. He'd

thought Griffith would see things between them couldn't work, just like he did. He'd thought Griffith would be sad but resigned, that he'd *see* that they couldn't be together. He seemed convinced he could find a way, though, and while Lawrence wanted to believe him, he realized how dangerous that was. "Don't you think I've already tried?"

Griffith frowned. "You no doubt have, but I'm a scientist. A geneticist. This is what I work on every day."

"I've already gone to doctors and geneticists. None of them were able to find a way for me to completely take the venom out of my body."

"You don't have to take it out. I'm guessing that the reason you can't entirely control the amount of venom in your saliva was that something is stopping you from doing this, probably a trigger or something. You were manipulated to become a weapon, right?"

Lawrence didn't like the analytical way Griffith was looking at him, but that was only because he wished Griffith would look at him with love and heat in his eyes. He'd do with this, though. At least Griffith wasn't trying to get him into bed or anything. "Yes."

"Then whoever did this to you will have wanted you to be ready to kill at all times. How long does it take you to lower or raise the amount of venom?"

Lawrence sighed. "I don't want to talk about this right now." He should have known better than to stay. Win had suggested someone else could keep an eye on Griffith, but Lawrence felt he needed to be the one to stand guard tonight.

Maybe it hadn't been such a good idea.

Griffith grinned. "That's fine. I need to think about this anyway. I *know* I can find a way to manipulate your genes to make it so that you can get rid of the venom entirely and only have it back when and if you want it."

Lawrence wanted to believe him. He was tempted to. But

he didn't want to give himself false hope like he had in the beginning when he'd realized what he'd become and he'd gone to all the doctors he could find. That was how the council had found him. One of the doctors had been working with them, and they'd reached out to Lawrence. Lawrence had found a purpose with them, a way to use what had been done to him in a good way.

Lawrence was lucky that the pizza arrived shortly after that. Griffith didn't even hear it—he was still sitting on the couch, his gaze unfocused as he no doubt thought about what Lawrence had told him. Lawrence could almost see the cogs turning in his brain. He was trying to find a way to free Lawrence from his curse, and Lawrence wanted to believe he could, maybe a little too much.

"Griffith?" he gently called out once he was back with the pizza box.

Griffith jerked as if Lawrence had yelled. "What?"

"Pizza is here."

"Oh. Good."

He didn't stop thinking, but Lawrence was glad for the silence. They ate on the couch, Griffith still lost in his thoughts, Lawrence fake-watching TV. He had no idea what was on, but it was better than staring at Griffith. It was what Lawrence wanted to do, but he knew he shouldn't get used to being with Griffith.

"You can call me Griff," Griffith said suddenly.

Lawrence had been paying attention to Griffith's presence, but he was still surprised. "Yes?"

"Yes. No one else calls me that, but I like it."

"I see." Lawrence wasn't sure it was a good idea—it was one more step toward an intimacy they couldn't afford—but if it was important to Griff, then he'd do it. "Some people call me Law. I know Lawrence is a mouthful."

"Well, it's certainly easier to think of you as Law when I'm mentally cursing you for not even wanting to try."

There they were again. "I want to try. Believe me. I've never wanted anything in my life as much as I want to be with you. I won't put you in danger because of it, though."

Griffith cleaned his fingers on his napkin and twisted sideways, sliding his leg under him. Lawrence was afraid to look at him. Griffith was stubborn, and Lawrence was starting to see that when he wanted something, he wouldn't take no for an answer.

"I want to suggest something, and I'd like you to listen to me."

"I can do that." Lawrence supposed it was the least he could do.

"Okay. So, I know you won't kiss me or do anything that requires clothes to come off."

"Or bonding."

"Or bonding, but trust me, I'm nowhere near ready to think about that. What I want, what I was trying to say, is that I'm more shaken than I'm letting show right now."

Lawrence's snake immediately perked up at the thought of their mate being in distress, but Lawrence was more critical. He understood why Griffith might be shaken, but he hadn't looked like it until now, and Lawrence wasn't yet sure where he was going with this. "I'm sorry you had to go through this."

"I've always known my father was an asshole, so it's not as much of a surprise as you might think. But I'd never seen him like this. I don't want to believe it, but I think you might be right when you say that he could have hurt me, or at the very least ask someone else to do it. He doesn't want me to stick my nose into his business, and he knows that as long as I know someone is being hurt, I'll do exactly that."

"You shouldn't."

"That's not what we're talking about right now. We can

fight over that tomorrow, okay?"

Lawrence had to press his lips together so he wouldn't smile. God, he could so easily fall for Griffith. "I suppose we can do that."

"What I'd like you to do tonight is sleep with me."

All the humor fled Lawrence. "We can't—"

"I never mentioned sex."

That stopped Lawrence in his track. "What?"

"I said, sleep, not have sex. I doubt you're going to slobber all over me while we sleep, and I don't want to be alone. If I'm honest, I'm not even up for sex. I want to cuddle. I want to feel like I'm not as alone as I feel."

"You're not alone."

"Then show that to me. Spend the night with me in my bed. I promise I won't try to seduce you. I don't share your conviction that there's nothing we can do to change the way your ability works, but that's not something I can deal with right now. I'll need to think and study, and possibly to examine you and your genes if you let me. Maybe your medical records?" He waved. "Anyway, that's not something I can do right now, and I don't want to push you. You already admitted we're mates, and that's good enough for me right now."

It shouldn't be. Griffith deserved everything, not the half relationship Lawrence could give him. But Griffith needed him tonight, and Lawrence wanted at least this. He wanted the memories for when Griffith would move on and find someone else to love him.

Lawrence would never forget Griffith. They were mates. He'd always feel the hole in his heart, and that was okay. It was how things went in this kind of situation.

"All right."

Griffith's eyes widened. "Really?"

"Yes. What you went through tonight couldn't have been easy, and I won't leave you alone if you're not feeling up to it."

Griffith's shoulders relaxed. "Thank you."

Lawrence nodded. "We should probably clean up?" He wasn't sure when Griffith would want to go to bed, but now that he'd agreed, he felt awkward. He didn't know how to behave. He and Griffith weren't together, but they were going to share a bed tonight. They were probably going to cuddle, and Lawrence couldn't wait. He wasn't sure how he'd react, though, and that scared him. Would it make it even harder to leave Griffith behind when the time came?

He supposed he was about to find out.

Griffith was pretty sure Lawrence had no idea what to do. He'd managed to surprise and shock him when he'd asked him to stay the night and cuddle, and that had been what he was aiming for, at least in part. He *did* feel like he needed someone with him, holding him. The thought of what his father might have done, might still do, to make sure he didn't talk to anyone about what he'd found out was even more terrifying, because it was his father he was thinking about. There was no love lost between them, but Griffith still had a hard time believing his *father* would hurt him.

He didn't doubt he might, though.

Now that he'd had time to think about it, he realized why Lawrence had been so angry. Griffith's father worked for the government, and if anyone found out what they were up to, there would be an uproar, both from humans and from shifters. Shifters had been integrated into the military and the government for decades. A lot of them had revealed themselves over the years. Everyone would stand to lose a lot if it came out that the government had sanctioned capturing or buying shifters and experimenting on them again.

Hadn't they already lived through that? Most humans

would be horrified, just like Griffith was, and things would get ugly. Griffith's father needed to make sure no one found out, and now that Griffith knew, he was probably going to try to make him keep his mouth shut. Griffith didn't know how yet, and he didn't want to find out.

He never wanted to see his father again. At this point, he barely cared if the man was killed, although he'd rather not have Lawrence do it. Whatever would happen between them, he doubted he'd be able to forget that his mate had killed his father, even though his father deserved it.

"The bathroom is over there," he said, pointing at the door that opened in his bedroom.

Lawrence blinked. "Thank you." He disappeared into the bathroom, and Griffith took the time to relax, or at least to try to.

He turned the blanket down on the bed and patted it, then took his watch off and left it on the nightstand. He turned off the big light on the ceiling, leaving on only the small one on his nightstand.

He hadn't been lying when he'd said he wouldn't push for anything more than a hug. He understood why Lawrence was so afraid, and while his mind couldn't wait to get to work on the problem and solve it, he realized that Lawrence wasn't merely an enigma to solve.

He'd been living with this for who knew how long. He'd kept himself away from people because he was afraid of hurting them. He'd stayed away from *Griffith* because he thought nothing could happen between them.

And maybe he was right. Griffith had tried to look and sound confident when they'd talked about it, and he did believe he could find a way to control the venom in Lawrence's saliva and make a bond between them possible, but he might be wrong. It wouldn't be the first time. He'd do whatever he had to in order to make it work, though. He'd find a way.

He wasn't letting Lawrence go, not over this.

Griffith had already made his decision. Now he just had to convince Lawrence of it. He didn't need sex or even kissing to fall in love with Lawrence and be happy with him. It *was* true that he yearned to feel Lawrence's lips on his, and that he thought that some things would probably be doable without causing harm to anyone, but this wasn't the right moment to experiment. He knew Lawrence was going to fight him tooth and nail because he didn't think that being together in that way would be fair to Griffith, but Griffith was going to show him it wasn't true.

So what if he aged and died while Lawrence stayed the way he was?

It would be sad, devastating, even, and Griffith couldn't think about what Lawrence would have to face, but was it fair to deny both of them years of happiness because of it? Especially when Griffith thought he could help? He wanted years with Lawrence, decades, and it was going to take a lot to make him change his mind.

"You look like your head is about to explode," Lawrence said as he came out of the bathroom. He was still wearing the clothes Griffith had loaned him, but the tips of the hair that fell in front of his face were damp, and when Griffith walked closer, he could smell toothpaste on Lawrence's breath.

"It might. I need to stop thinking, but I always have a hard time doing that," Griffith said.

"I can see that. The bathroom is available."

Griffith was afraid to go inside. He was afraid Lawrence would take that opportunity to disappear and that his bedroom would be empty when he went back.

Of course, Lawrence seemed to understand that. Griffith wasn't sure how he did it, but the how didn't matter. "I'll still be here," Lawrence said in a quiet voice.

Griffith relaxed. "Thank you."

"You asked me to stay, and I said I would. I'm not going anywhere." He didn't have to add the *for now* for Griffith to hear it.

He had his work cut out for him, didn't he? Lawrence was going to fight him every step of the way because he thought it was the right thing to do, and Griffith was going to have to show him it wasn't.

Griffith rushed through taking a quick shower — he needed to get the sliminess of his father's words off his skin — and brushing his teeth. No matter what Lawrence had said, the fear that the bedroom would be empty when Griffith went back was still there.

He shouldn't have been worried, though. Lawrence was by the window when Griffith stumbled back into the bedroom, almost falling on his face in his haste. He was looking out, but he turned to look at Griffith, and Griffith didn't miss the way his eyes widened.

Griffith looked down at himself. "I hate sleeping in clothes. They twist around me. But I can put on a t-shirt if it makes you more comfortable." Griffith had put on pants, but he'd skipped the t-shirt, not because he was trying to seduce Lawrence — although if that worked, he wouldn't protest — but because he was more comfortable this way.

"It's fine. We're just going to sleep, right?"

Griffith hoped his smile was reassuring. "Right. Do you have a favorite side?"

"The one by the door, if that's okay with you."

Probably so he could act quickly if someone came in. The thought of Lawrence thinking about protecting him made Griffith's heart feel all gooey and warm.

Things got more awkward and tense when they settled into bed. Lawrence might as well have been a slat of wood since he held himself about as relaxed as one. His arms were straight by his sides, and he was staring at the ceiling. Griffith could see his eyes gleam in the light that came in from the window.

He didn't know how to get Lawrence to relax. He'd promised he wouldn't try anything, and he wouldn't, but he wasn't sure Lawrence believed him, and he did want them to be closer. "Can I move?" he asked. He was whispering because it felt like the right thing to do, like he'd jar the moment if he didn't.

"Of course."

"I meant, can I come closer. I promise not to try to kiss you or to touch you inappropriately. I just need . . . ."

"You need to be held."

"Yes, please. If that's okay with you. And I *can* put a shirt on if you're uncomfortable."

"You're fine." Lawrence rolled toward Griffith. "I'm just not sure . . ."

Griffith reached for Lawrence. He was the bigger one, and he pulled Lawrence close, settling him against his side. Lawrence slotted there as if he were made for it, with his head in the crook of Griffith's neck. Griffith felt him exhale and finally relax, and he couldn't resist placing a kiss on the top of Lawrence's head. His hair was soft and smelled of violet. It wasn't a scent Griffith would have picked for himself, but it was incredibly good. "This okay?" he asked.

Lawrence nodded. He tangled their legs together, and Griffith felt something settle in his chest.

This was where he belonged, where they *both* belonged, and Griffith was going to do everything in his power to make sure they could have this for the rest of their lives.

However long that was.

CHAPTER SIX

Lawrence was in trouble.

He'd known this would happen as soon as he'd first seen Griffith, and his impression had been confirmed when he'd started spending time with Griffith.

He was falling in love with his mate.

Griffith was infuriatingly stubborn. He'd made it his mission to show Lawrence that they could work together, even with Lawrence's curse.

Griffith had managed to get Win to tell him where the warehouse was, and he visited as often as his job made it possible. He hadn't talked about going back to his parents' house, thank God, but Lawrence was still on his guard. There was no way White would let anyone get away with knowing what he was doing, not even his son, and Lawrence would be ready for him when he or one of his cronies came for Griffith.

He might not be planning to bond with Griffith, but that didn't change the fact that he and Griffith were mates, and Lawrence was going to keep him safe. He would have even if they weren't mates. Griffith was precious. He was stubborn, but that helped him in his job. He'd chosen his field to help people, and he did, even though it took a long time for him to unravel the secrets of people's genes.

And he wasn't trying to help only through his job. When he was at the warehouse, he was always helping someone — Graham with his cooking, Payne with his math homework, Rocco with whatever it was he did when he didn't have to patch up people. Griffith had even tried to comfort Beck recently when he hadn't heard from Armand, who had been sent to infiltrate White's lab. He'd taken the place of one of the scientists, and since he *wasn't* one, everyone was afraid for him. He might be able to keep up the pretense for a bit, but there was no way he'd manage if he had to do actual science, even though Griffith had coached him through a few things before he'd left.

Griffith just fit in, and it was too easy for Lawrence to imagine he was there to stay.

The door to the kitchen opened. Lawrence hadn't been reading the book he was holding, and he looked up, distracted. He just had the time to see a flurry of movement that resembled Beck as he threw himself against the person walking in. There was a screech that made everyone in the room wince, and Lawrence realized what had happened.

Armand was home.

Everything was a flurry of voices and movements for a while. Everyone wanted to talk to Armand, but they gave him and Beck space until Win arrived. Then Win took over, dragging Armand into his office for a report. Beck went right along with him, and Lawrence tried to get back to his book. He was relieved, and it was easier to focus on the words now that he knew that all of his family was safe.

Of course, his peace didn't last long.

"What do you think he found out?" Ulric asked as he flopped onto the couch next to Lawrence.

"No idea."

"Do you think Win will let us know?"

"Probably."

Ulric huffed. "You're no fun. Have you talked to Griffith yet? Because to me, it doesn't look like you've managed to convince him to keep his distance."

Lawrence groaned and closed his book. "Do you have to stick your nose into this? It's none of your business."

Ulric stretched out. "Except it is, because you're my best friend and you're being an idiot."

Lawrence wasn't going to be able to read, was he? He'd hoped to get a few chapters in before Griffith arrived—and he *would* come—but Ulric wasn't going to allow him to. "You know what I can do."

Ulric rolled his eyes. "We all do, and so does Griffith. I don't see him keeping his distance. He's surprisingly affectionate with you, considering that you're an emotional hedgehog."

"I haven't been able to convince him that we can't have a future," Lawrence grumbled.

"That's what I'm talking about. I know you can't bond, but he's not so old that you already have to worry about him aging, and I know he's been working on a way to fix you."

"I'm not broken."

"You're right, you're not. You're different. We all are. But you got the short stick, and I'm glad you found Griffith. He's the perfect guy for you. He's going to make sure you don't retreat inside your shell and push him away, and he won't stop until he finds a way to help you and to be able to bond with you. He's also going to take care of you, which is something a lot of us want to do."

"I don't need to be taken care of."

Ulric's smile was sad as he patted Lawrence's thigh. "We all do sometimes, and that's okay. It's what makes us human, and it would be too easy to forget that we're also that. We don't just deal with being shifters. We also have to deal with being different than we were growing up, and I don't know about you, but some days, I still wish I'd never ended up in that lab."

Of course Lawrence still wished that. He was pretty sure all of them did.

"Give him a chance, Law," Ulric murmured. "We all love

you here, but he's different. He's your mate. I know you're scared for him, and I understand why you are, but if there's one person who can help you, it's him. You have to let him, though."

Lawrence wasn't sure what to say. He'd been to so many doctors, and none of them had been able to help him. Even Rocco had tried, although he was a healer rather than a geneticist. But Lawrence was still the same as he was when he'd left the lab. He was still venomous, and he wasn't sure he could bring himself to hope that might change one day only to be disappointed and to have to give up a future with Griffith.

When the door opened again and Win, Roark, Beck, and Armand walked in, almost everyone in the warehouse was in the kitchen or the living room. They wanted to know what had happened and if they'd finally be able to do something, to help the shifters and possibly the humans that were in White's lab and to set fire to it.

"Meeting?" Graham asked from the kitchen. He was wearing an apron and holding a wooden spoon.

Win nodded. "Meeting. Is everyone here?"

"Miles is still out on that job," Ulric said. "And I think Tony went out."

"We'll bring them up to speed later. All right. Everyone, listen up. As you know, Armand went undercover as one of White's scientists."

"How did he manage not to get caught?" Ulric asked in a whisper.

Lawrence rolled his eyes. "He knows how to do his job."

"Yeah, but come on. I know *I* wouldn't have been able to fake being a scientist. When your mate starts talking about his job, I fall asleep."

"Shut up and listen to Win."

" —entire team of scientists working there," Win was

saying. "From what Armand found out, we were right. They're working on making the perfect soldier, a killing machine. They're pretty much doing what was done to you, although they're also working on a way to control the shifters they have."

"Can't have a war machine that doesn't obey," Ulric grumbled.

"What do we do now?" Lawrence asked instead of telling Ulric to shut up again.

"Well, I have to talk this over with the council, of course. Armand has a list of names, but he wasn't able to find out who in the government gave the okay for this project, and that's something we need to know. I also don't know if the council will use the enforcers rather than us in this case. We're not trained for rescue missions, not the way they are. We're the guys who take out the bad people."

"I want to see this through," Lawrence said. He agreed that they probably weren't the best choice, but it had gotten personal when he'd realized Griffith was his mate, and this was one way to make sure Griffith would be safe.

"We all do. This started with us, even though White and his team weren't involved in the group trying to kill us. But we discovered this, and we better than most can understand what the shifters in that lab are going through and what they'll have to face once they get out. I'll mention it to the council, and hopefully, they'll agree to have us help. The enforcers know how to keep secrets, so I hope we'll be able to work with them to take down White and his people."

Shit. That was what Lawrence wanted, and he would make sure he didn't have a hand in whatever happened to Griffith's father, but he was going to have to tell him about this, and he wasn't looking forward to it.

Griffith was beat. He'd been working overtime on helping Lawrence while still doing what he was being paid to do, and juggling the two wasn't easy. He was making it work, though, and going back to the warehouse after a long day of work always made him feel better. He hadn't moved in yet, and Lawrence was keeping his distance, but Griffith was pretty sure he was wearing him down.

Lawrence would probably never agree to bond or even kiss Griffith, not until Griffith found a way to neutralize his venom, but Griffith hadn't lost hope yet. He'd been thinking about a way to get closer to Lawrence ever since they'd spent the night in his bed a few weeks ago—and to wear Lawrence down. He knew Lawrence wanted him as much as he wanted Lawrence, and he hated that they could barely touch each other because of Lawrence's fear.

Griffith understood what was at stake. Lawrence had agreed to let him work on him, and he'd taken samples and studied the files Rocco had given him. He knew what he was up against. He was aware of the fact that a bit too much venom could kill him if he didn't have the antivenom with him, and yes, that thought was petrifying. But he didn't want this to be the thing that would keep him from being with Lawrence. They could find a way around it—closed mouth kisses, cuddling, hell, maybe even a hand job or a blowjob, as long as Lawrence wore a condom. Lawrence just needed to understand that Griffith wasn't underestimating his condition.

Griffith was surprised when he walked into the warehouse kitchen—he'd been given the codes needed to enter the building, so he didn't have to call anyone to open the door for him—and saw everyone was there, or at least he thought so. He still tended to lose count since there were so many people who lived there.

That thought infuriated him. Those people, Lawrence and his friends, had been dealt a shitty hand in life. They'd been taken from their homes and hurt, and Griffith's father was doing it again, hurting people who hadn't done anything, who didn't deserve it. Not that anyone deserved to have anything like his father was doing done to them. Griffith's father was a monster, and Griffith couldn't wait until he was arrested and his mother was finally free of him. He'd stayed away from the house, and his mom hadn't called him again. She probably wouldn't, not after what had happened during that dinner. It was a relief not to have to make small talk when Griffith knew what his father was doing.

Everyone turned toward the door when it shut. Griffith blinked and waved. "Am I missing something?" he asked, looking for Lawrence in the crowd. He found his mate on the couch, Ulric next to him.

"We're in a meeting," Win explained.

"Do you need me to leave?"

"Of course not. You actually might be able to help, although we should probably go to my office to discuss it later. It would be useless to get too technical here."

If Win wanted to talk to Griffith, that meant he needed to talk about whatever experiment his father was doing. Griffith wasn't looking forward to it, but he'd listen, and he'd help if he could. "Of course."

Griffith made his way toward the couch. Ulric moved to the side so Griffith could sit between him and Lawrence. Griffith dumped his messenger bag onto the coffee table and settled down, trying to be as quiet as he could. "What's going on?" he asked.

"Armand is back," Lawrence told him.

Griffith wasn't sure how he'd managed to miss Armand, since he was back to his usual long hair and colorful tattoos. He'd known the man was undercover at his father's lab since he'd helped him build up some knowledge about the experiments. "Is he okay?"

"Looks like he was able to blend in well enough."

"What's the council going to do about the people behind this?" someone asked.

Griffith felt a little lost, but he could ask more questions later.

"I still don't know," Win said. "They've been talking about different options, but since we don't know who exactly is behind this, it's hard to make a choice. We need to find out how high and deep it goes. Depending on who is involved, the decision will be different."

"What about my father?" Griffith asked. *Damn it.* Everyone turned to look at him. He cleared his throat. "I want him to pay just as much as all of you. I just, well, he's my father. I'd like to have a chance to wrap my mind around things before they happen if it's possible."

Win's smile was kind. He'd never held the fact that Griffith's father was hurting shifters against Griffith, and neither had anyone else there. "I'll let you know as soon as I find out. But you probably suspect what the council will decide."

Griffith could. He'd known his father would probably be killed by one of the assassins ever since he'd realized that was what Lawrence was. He wasn't sure how to feel about it, but he understood it wasn't his place to make this decision. He wasn't the one being hurt. He wasn't the one locked in a lab.

He needed to help, but he wasn't sure how. "What's going to happen to the rest of the lab and the scientists? I mean, I expect you're going to free the shifters there, which is great, and you're going to do whatever it is you need to do to my father." Which was less great, but Griffith would learn to deal with it. "But what about the scientists there? Are you going to . . . take care of all of them? And the people behind it? Considering what we're talking about, they're probably powerful enough to stay hidden or to find a way out, or maybe even to turn things in a way that will make the council seem at fault.

I know you guys are used to dealing with this kind of stuff, but it's something to think about." Griffith needed to keep Lawrence safe. That was his first objective, and he'd do just about anything to make it happen.

"What are you suggesting?"

Griffith had thought about it, so he knew how to answer. "Go public."

Win frowned. "Public?"

"Stay anonymous, of course, but depending on who is behind this and on how well-known they are, it might be the best way to make sure it doesn't happen again. You don't think the higher-ups are in on this, right?"

"No. The council regularly works with some of the officials, and they don't think so."

"But you can't deny those people would probably know about this and that they won't want the public to find out. It would make them look bad. They're going to try to brush everything under the rug, and that means that it could happen again. I don't expect anyone to be aware of everything that happens in every branch of the military. How do we make it so that it doesn't, then? How do you make it so that even the people who will manage to wiggle their way out of a punishment pay? You show the world what's going on."

Win didn't look convinced. "They're going to be pissed if we do that."

"So? It's not like we're talking about something trivial. *They* were the ones who betrayed the council and shifters in the first place. I'm not one for vengeance or whatever, but I think this would be the best way to get people's attention, hold them accountable, and to make sure it doesn't happen again." Griffith shrugged. "Just a thought. But people deserve to know what's going on, even if they weren't involved."

"I'll bring it up during the next council meeting. Thank you for your point of view." Win looked around. "I'll call for another meeting as soon as I know more. We're going to be involved in this, though. I promise you that. I might not have been through what you all have been and are still going through, but I spent time in a lab, and no one should ever go through that. White and his people chose the wrong shifters to mess with."

There was some cheering, and even Griffith clapped. He might feel conflicted about all of this, but of one thing he was sure—his father shouldn't have even thought about doing this, let alone done it. He was going to pay for it, as was right, and the shifters who were in his cages would be freed.

Lawrence kept an eye on Griffith during dinner. He'd just been told his father was probably going to be executed for what he'd done to shifters. There was no way he was taking it as well as it looked. Of course, that wasn't exactly what Win had said, but everyone knew what he'd implied—and what the council would decide. This was the only way they could get White to stop doing what he was doing indefinitely. They'd tried going along with the humans in the beginning, handing over the humans who were hurting shifters to them, but those people always ended up free after only a few years, and they went back to their old ways. That hadn't been acceptable then, and it wasn't now.

But Griffith didn't even seem to care. He was talking and even laughing as they ate at the dining table, and he looked like he belonged there.

"You look like a worried mother hen," Ulric teased.

Lawrence kicked him under the table. "You'd be worried too if you were me."

"Probably. He's taking it too well, huh?"

"Yeah."

Ulric leaned back in his chair. "You know, not everyone

has a good relationship with their family like you do. From the little Griffith told me, it's obvious his relationship with his father has always been conflicted. I don't think it's that weird for him to accept the thought that his father is going to be killed because, well, the guy isn't a nice man, and because he doesn't have that big of a part in Griffith's life as it is. I'm not saying you shouldn't keep an eye on him to make sure he's okay, but the loss of a father isn't that big of a deal for some people."

Lawrence knew Ulric spoke from experience, so he squeezed his friend's arm. "Thank you."

"No worries. And you should rethink the not having sex rules you have with Griff. He's looking at you like he wants to eat you," Ulric said, his voice barely louder than a whisper.

He was right. When Lawrence looked up, Griffith was staring at him with an intensity that Lawrence had seen in his eyes only when he talked about his work or the kids he volunteered with at the shelter. It was a different kind of look, but it was just as intense, and it made Lawrence want to squirm in his chair. "I can't," he murmured.

Ulric sighed. "I know why, and I get it, but come on. There has to be a way. Liquid latex? I know it's a thing."

"And I don't want to find out how you know that." There was no way Lawrence was using liquid latex, but he couldn't deny he wanted Griffith as much as Griffith seemed to want him.

Griffith had been staying at the warehouse almost every night since the night they'd spent in his apartment after he talked to his father. There was no escaping him, and Lawrence hadn't tried to—he didn't *want* to try. He wanted Griffith, and he was more than happy to have him in his bed every night. The only thing they did was cuddling and sleeping tangled together, but it wasn't enough.

Lawrence wanted more. He wanted *everything*, no matter

how impossible that was.

He'd known this was going to be hard when he'd gone into it, but he hadn't realized *how* hard.

"You should probably stop looking at him like you're about to fuck him on the dinner table," Ulric suggested, humor in his voice.

Lawrence groaned. "What the fuck am I doing, Ulric? I've never wanted anyone the way I want him, but I can't have him. I hate my life."

"But you *can* have him. Come on, Law. He's a scientist. I know he's already working in a way to get into your pants and bond with you, and I have enough experience with sex to know there's stuff you can do without spilling blood or anything else where it can hurt him. I know the thought of hurting him is terrifying and that you've been holding back, but give the two of you a chance to at least try to work something out, yeah?"

Lawrence's first instinct was to say no. The thought of hurting Griffith was enough to make Lawrence need to take a step back and stay away from him. He couldn't deny the two of them couldn't do this for much longer, though. Griffith was pushing for more than sharing a bed, and Lawrence wanted that as much as his mate did. Could he risk it, though? Could he put his mate's life in danger just because they wanted to make out?

"You need to talk to the guy," Ulric pointed out before stuffing his mouth with carrots.

"I already have."

"Then talk again." Or at least that was what Lawrence thought he was saying, since his mouth was full.

Maybe he was right. It was obvious that what was between Griffith and Lawrence wasn't working, or rather, that it wasn't enough anymore. Lawrence had two options — talk to Griffith again and try to work through this, or leave and never look back.

He knew he couldn't do that. He couldn't leave his job and the family he'd built here. He didn't *want* to leave Griffith.

Goddammit. He'd let himself fall in love with the man, and now there was no going back because it would hurt both of them. Lawrence wasn't sure where that left him, both of them, but he supposed he was going to find out soon. Griffith had probably already caught how uneasy Lawrence was, and Lawrence knew an interrogation was coming. For once, he didn't mind. He was afraid, but he could deal with it—or at least he hoped so.

He was glad when Griffith didn't jump to the conversation right away. They hung around with the others for a bit longer, and Lawrence didn't have to ask him if he was staying. He was. He had been ever since that first night, and Lawrence hadn't protested because he didn't want to be away from his mate.

Maybe there was hope for them after all. Lawrence wanted to believe it. He still wasn't sure he could, though.

"You're quiet tonight," Griffith said as they climbed the stairs to Lawrence's room. Griffith hadn't been staying in the guest room he'd used that first night even though Win had offered it to him.

"I was thinking."

"About? Or would you rather not talk about it?"

"I'm worried about you." This was the easiest bit to confess.

"Because of my father?"

"Yes. I don't know. I can't help but think that maybe you don't understand what's going to happen to him."

Griffith waited to answer until they were back in Lawrence's room with the door closed behind them. He leaned against it and peered at Lawrence. "I *do* realize what Win was saying. He's going to task one of you to kill my father, probably sooner rather than later, once he and the council have the answers they need. And that's okay."

"He's your father."

"Biologically, yes, sure. He provided half of my genes. But he's never been a father, and he's never been a good husband to my mother. I grew up with him, yet I don't know him, and what I do know of him, I hate. He's a monster. He's been abusing and using my mother for decades. He hates me, and he hasn't had any problem letting me know. He thinks I'm an abomination." Griffith shook his head. "He's never been a father, and I can't excuse what he's been doing. He *deserves* to die. Some people do, and there's no changing that. I hate what this is going to do to my mother, but it has to be done. I'm a hundred percent okay with it. I've had more than enough time to wrap my mind around it and accept it. You don't have to worry about me. I'll be okay."

Lawrence knew he had to believe him, but he couldn't help but be worried about him. "You know you can talk to me about this, right?"

"I know. I don't want to, though."

"Because you think it will hurt me, because of my past." It *was* true that Lawrence would be more than happy to kill Griffith's father, even though he hadn't been the one to make him what he was now. That didn't mean he couldn't care for his mate's feelings and comfort him, though.

Griffith pushed away from the door and came to stand in front of Lawrence. "I want to kiss you. Please."

Griffith never meant to push Lawrence, but maybe it was time to. He'd been patient. He'd given Lawrence time to get used to his presence, to having him in his life. He'd given Lawrence time to fall in love with him, and he hoped that had happened, because he'd fallen hard and fast for Lawrence.

Griffith knew it was the bond, but he'd never wanted any-one the way he wanted Lawrence, and he wasn't going to let something like Lawrence's ability stop him from getting what he wanted. He'd find a way around it, and around Lawrence's hesitation.

He needed Lawrence to say yes right now, though.

He swallowed. "I want you to say yes. We'll keep our lips closed so there won't be any saliva swap. I promise."

He expected Lawrence to say no. He wouldn't have been surprised if he had. He knew how careful Lawrence always was about this, even though he thought it was overkill a lot of the time.

"All right."

Griffith blinked. "All right?"

"Yes. Mouths closed, though."

"I swear." But Griffith was going to find a way to control the venom, dammit. He needed Lawrence like he needed air, and stamp kisses weren't going to make it for long.

He carefully reached for Lawrence, pulling him into his arms the way he did every night they shared a bed. Lawrence shuddered. That was enough to tell Griffith he was as anxious and nervous as him, and it made him feel better. Lawrence might be careful to keep distance between them, but he was doing it because of the venom, not because he didn't want Griffith. Griffith knew he wanted him. The obstacle between them wasn't their feelings. It was the damn venom.

Lawrence slotted against Griffith's chest, his arms going around Griffith's neck while Griffith wrapped his around Lawrence's waist. He leaned down, holding his breath and half expecting Lawrence to change his mind and move away, but he didn't. No, he stayed right where he was in Griffith's arms and allowed Griffith to press their lips together.

Griffith wanted more. He wanted to lose himself in

Lawrence, to learn his body inch by inch, to make him crazy. He didn't. He'd promised Lawrence he would limit himself to this, and as hard as it was, he did. Lawrence trusted him, and he wasn't going to break that trust.

He smiled and rubbed the tips of their noses together. "How was that?" His voice was slightly hoarse, telling Lawrence how he felt if Lawrence was able to read it.

"Perfect," Lawrence said, and he sounded as wrecked as Griffith felt.

Griffith nodded. He didn't want to push, but he wanted so much more, and he knew they could both stay safe even if they pushed themselves further than this. "Trust me?"

Lawrence's lips twitched. "What do you have in mind?"

Griffith dropped to his knees. Lawrence's eyes widened, but he didn't push Griffith away, and he didn't ask him to stop. Griffith wasn't sure why, but he wasn't going to hesitate. He'd been dreaming of this for what felt like forever, even though it had only been a few weeks.

He reached into his pocket and took out the condom he'd been carrying around—just in case. He held it up so that Lawrence could see it. He'd no doubt realized what Griffith was about to do because of it and Griffith's position, which was good. Griffith wanted him to say no if he didn't want to. He hoped he wouldn't, though. He didn't want fear to stop them, not when there was no reason to, not when he knew what he was going against and when he was going to be careful.

"Everything will be all right. I know what I'm doing," Griffith promised. He'd do everything he could to keep that promise, too. He wanted Lawrence to be comfortable and to forget why he thought they shouldn't do this. He wanted to show him that this would work and that they could be together in more ways than they had until now. He'd find a way to neutralize the venom sooner or later, but in the meantime, he wanted everything they could have, and he suspected

Lawrence felt the same way.

He dropped the condom to the floor and cupped his hands around Lawrence's calves. They were hard with muscles and tension, but Lawrence didn't say anything. He continued to look down at Griffith as Griffith ran his hands upward, stroking Lawrence's thighs. He hooked his fingers in the loops of Lawrence's jeans and gently pulled. The jeans stayed right where they were.

Griffith grinned. "You're not going to help me even a little bit?" he asked.

"I thought you didn't want me to move." There was teasing in Lawrence's voice, and it helped Griffith relax even more.

Lawrence *did* want this. He was willing to try, and that was enough to make Griffith feel all fluttery inside. Pretty much everything Lawrence did or said made Griffith feel that way, but this moment was special.

Griffith reached for the button of Lawrence's jeans. Holding his breath, he slid it open. Lawrence's jeans gently sagged on his hips, and this time, when Griffith pulled, they went down.

Lawrence's skin was covered with fine blond hair that tickled and prickled Griffith's palms when he stroked his thighs. Lawrence was wearing a pair of tight black boxer briefs, and his cock was highlighted perfectly. It was starting to plump, and even though he wanted to get right to sucking him, Griffith knew Lawrence would be more comfortable if he kept the fabric barrier between them until he could put the condom on him.

He ran his fingertips along Lawrence's length, smiling when his cock twitched in answer. Yes, Lawrence liked this. He wanted this as much as Griffith did.

Griffith pressed harder against Lawrence's cock. He played with the length, never touching the skin. He wanted to taste it, suck on the head he could feel and see under the fabric, but that would be going too fast, and he didn't want to end the evening in the infirmary downstairs. That would only make Lawrence feel guilty, and he'd close off even harder than he had before.

"You're beautiful," Griffith murmured.

"You can't really see me."

"Trust me, I've never forgotten that day when you shifted in my car when you were in my apartment. Your body is seared into my mind, and you *are* beautiful."

"That's why you like me?"

"Not only." Griffith squeezed Lawrence's cock and leaned closer, pressing a kiss against the soft skin of his stomach. Lawrence was hard with muscles all over, including there, but the skin was smooth and called for Griffith's lips. "You're trying so hard to do the right thing. You're worried about my father because he's my father, even though you hate him. You want to help people. You've been doing that for years without resting, without allowing yourself to get close to anyone because you didn't want to put them in danger. But you can stop doing that. I *know* what I'm up against, and I'm up for the challenge. I promise you, everything is going to be okay."

With that, Griffith grabbed the elastic band on Lawrence's underwear and pulled it. He took extra care not to touch Lawrence as he lowered his boxer briefs down his legs, exposing him. His cock was as slender as he was, with the hair at its base blond and well-trimmed.

Griffith moved forward. He felt Lawrence tense, but he limited himself to blowing on the head of his cock, smiling when Lawrence shuddered. He wanted Lawrence to forget that he thought they shouldn't be doing this. He wanted him to enjoy the moment without obsessing over what-ifs.

He took the condom from the floor and opened it. He rolled it over Lawrence's cock, still careful not to touch the beading semen at the slit. Lawrence visibly relaxed once he was covered, and Griffith knew he felt better. He probably shouldn't have teased him the way he had, but damn, it had felt so good, even though he hadn't even been touching him.

"Ready?" he asked, just to be sure.

Lawrence nodded tightly, and Griffith didn't hesitate. He moved closer and opened his mouth, wrapping his lips around the head of Lawrence's cock and gently sucking. Lawrence hissed and buried his hands into Griffith's hair. Griffith didn't mind a bit of hair pulling now and then, and he grinned up at Lawrence. Lawrence rolled his eyes, a sure sign that Griffith needed to focus on what he was doing with his mouth first.

It had been a while since Griffith had blown anyone. His jaw started to ache almost right away, and he had to stop too often to breathe, but Lawrence didn't seem to care. He was moving his hips as if unable to stop himself, and his fingers tightened in Griffith's hair.

Griffith was hard in his pants, but he focused on Lawrence. This was for him, to show him that they could do this, that they *could* have some of the things other couples had. Sex wasn't indispensable for Griffith, and he could easily do without, but he wanted to give Lawrence the world — and a blowjob.

The sounds coming out of Lawrence's mouth, the way he smelled and moved, made it worth the ache in Griffith's jaw. He tried to focus on the head so he wouldn't have to be in too much pain, and he wrapped his fingers around the base of Lawrence's cock, jacking him as he sucked.

Lawrence's hips jerked. He moaned, and Griffith tongued the slit of his cock through the condom. He wished he could taste Lawrence even though he'd never been particularly fond of the taste of cum. Lawrence's cock twitched in Griffith's mouth, and Griffith almost bit down. He stayed still, though, allowing Lawrence to move in and out of his mouth at the pace he preferred.

It was the right choice. Lawrence filled the condom after a few more thrusts into Griffith's mouth. Griffith could feel the warmth of his semen through the condom, and he gently moved away. He knew Lawrence was going to want to be the one taking care of the condom, and that was okay.

He needed a moment to wrap his mind around what had just happened anyway.

CHAPTER SEVEN

"Do you really think it worked?" Lawrence asked. He didn't feel any different, but then, he hadn't felt different even right after the scientists had played with his genes.

He'd been wary of allowing Griffith to do the same, not because he didn't trust Griffith—he did, and with his life—but because he didn't want to have to go through that again. He hadn't wanted to feel like a lab rat, but Griffith had made the process gentle, maybe even loving. He'd explained everything to Lawrence as he worked, even though Lawrence had understood less than half of it. It had been reassuring, though.

This moment wasn't. It was the make-it-or-break-it moment, and Lawrence wasn't sure what he wanted to happen.

He and Griffith had learned to live together. Griffith had moved in with Lawrence soon after they'd first had sex. Knowing that was possible, having Griffith do it, had made Lawrence realize that while he did have to be careful, he'd allowed his curse to control his life and his feelings. He hadn't allowed himself to be with anyone, to become close even to his friends, because of the fear he had of hurting them. Griffith had blown through that fear and had shown Lawrence that he could have more.

And he did. Griffith shared his room, and they went to bed together every night. They woke up together every morning, something Lawrence had never thought he could have. Griffith was there when he came back from the missions Win sent him on, welcoming him back and making him feel loved every step of the way in the life they were building together.

Nothing had been done about Griffith's father yet. The council needed more answers, more certainties, and it was taking a while to get all that. They were keeping an eye on White, and he'd scaled down whatever he was doing in his lab, but Lawrence hated every second they had to leave those shifters there. He knew it was the best way to do this, though. Going in there with guns blazing and getting the shifters out of there would only solve part of the problem. The lab, everyone who worked there, and the people who'd authorized it and were funding it, needed to be eradicated so that no other shifters would be hurt.

"Law? I promise I know what I'm doing," Griffith said.

Law licked his lips. "I know. I wouldn't have allowed you to do it otherwise."

Griffith nodded and pushed the files he was holding toward Lawrence. "There's no trace of venom in your saliva or your blood right now."

"That could change."

"Of course it could. You have the ability to control it, though. You've trained long enough to be sure of yourself, and I know you won't hurt me. It *worked*, Law. It worked, and we can bond."

Lawrence had thought it would take Griffith a lot longer to be able to do this. He'd told Rocco to give Griffith everything he needed, including old exams results and the files that Lawrence had retrieved from the lab when he'd left. Griffith had found everything that had been done to Lawrence in those, and somehow, he'd managed to find a way to modify Lawrence slightly so that he could suppress the venom. It had something to do with his control over the venom sacks, but when Griffith had tried to explain things in details, Lawrence had understood only half of it.

The how or why didn't matter to him. Now Lawrence could control the venom. He couldn't do it for long, only a few days at a time before he had to open the sacks and let it out, but Griffith was confident that Lawrence could learn to do it for months at a time if he gave himself time. He hadn't been able to get Lawrence back to being just a shifter, and he'd apologized for that, but Lawrence wasn't sure he would have wanted that even if the possibility had been on the table. He wouldn't be an assassin anymore if he were just another shifter, and his job meant a lot to him.

"Come on, Law. You've managed to control the venom for the past two days. I've been immunizing myself with your venom, just in case something *does* go wrong. Nothing will, though. I'm sure of it." He took Lawrence's hand and squeezed. "This is my job. I'm good at it. And I want to bond with you."

For some reason, bonding was much scarier than having sex. Lawrence and Griffith had found their way to a healthy, satisfying sex life. The fear of hurting Griffith was always in the back of Lawrence's mind, but he trusted Griffith, and Griffith trusted him. They loved each other, and Lawrence couldn't wait to spend the rest of his life with Griffith.

But fuck, Lawrence was terrified.

Still, Griffith had shown him that they could have everything together if only Lawrence trusted him and himself, and Lawrence did.

He dropped the files to the floor and climbed into Griffith's lap. Griffith's smile was triumphant and smug, and Lawrence laughed, kissing him. He was still wary of opening his mouth and welcoming Griffith's tongue when they did this, but it was probably the best way to make sure Griffith would be okay. If there really was no venom in Lawrence's saliva, Griffith would be fine, and they could go ahead with the bonding.

So he kissed Griffith again, opening his lips and drawing Griffith's tongue into his mouth. Griffith made a pleased sound and sank against Lawrence, hugging him close and stroking his back.

Lawrence wanted this for the rest of his life. He wanted Griffith to be by his side in thirty, forty, fifty years. He wanted them to age together and to build a life. He wouldn't be an assassin forever. He wanted to make Griffith happy.

He moved back and looked Griffith in the eyes. Griffith's lips shone with their saliva, and he looked healthy. He *was* healthy. Nothing was going to change that. Lawrence was holding the venom in, and he'd continue to do so even through their bonding.

He licked his lips and eyed Griffith's neck. Then he reached for the nightstand. He'd left a knife there, knowing what Griffith would want. He grabbed it and raised it to his neck—he didn't have claws when he shifted so he couldn't use one to open a wound—but Griffith stopped him, taking it out of his hands. "I'll do this," he said.

Lawrence could see a wariness in his gaze, but his hand was steady when he held the knife up to Lawrence's neck. The blade bit into Lawrence's flesh, but it was quick, and even though it burned, Lawrence only had to focus on what was about to happen to forget the pain.

Griffith leaned forward. Lawrence closed his eyes as Griffith's lips sealed around the wound. There was a pull on the wound, and Lawrence knew Griffith was drinking his blood.

He stopped resisting.

He tilted his head a bit more, grabbed the back of Griffith's head, and bit down with fangs that felt odd in his human mouth. Blood filled his mouth, tasting like the future they'd have together and the love they shared. Lawrence had thought he could never have this, that if he ever met his mate, he'd have to push him away for his safety. Yet here he was, binding his life to Griffith, making them one forever.

He felt the bond seal, and he focused on what Griffith was feeling, praying he wouldn't be sick.

He wasn't. Even as they slowly moved apart, the only things that Lawrence could feel through the bond were happiness and love. He'd known Griffith loved him, but he'd never realized how much. Griffith had been ready to do anything for him, to show him they could be together like this, and Lawrence was glad he'd given in, that he'd listened to Griffith and that he'd given them a chance.

Griffith smiled. "See? It wasn't that bad."

"You're okay?" Lawrence knew the venom was still in the sacks where it was created. He was keeping it there. He needed to be sure, though.

Griffith's smile widened. "I've never felt better."

Lawrence breathed out in relief. "Good."

Griffith reached for him, and Lawrence felt the spark of lust through the bond, but before they could do anything about that, someone knocked on the door. "Law? Is Griffith in there with you?" Ulric called out.

"I hope you have a damn good reason to interrupt our bonding," Lawrence called back.

"Shit. Sorry. I didn't mean to, but Win wants to see everyone."

That was probably the one reason Lawrence would be glad Ulric had come. "What did he say?" he asked, scrambling to get to the door and open it.

Ulric's gaze went right to Lawrence's neck, and he grinned. "Congrats."

"Thanks, and now tell me what Win said."

Ulric sobered. "We're going in, man. We're going to rescue those shifters."

Excerpt

"You busy?"

Harrison looked up from his computer. "Nope."

Jordan arched a brow. "Aren't you doing paperwork?"

"That's what I said. Not busy."

"Someone has to do that paperwork."

"I will. Just not now since you seem to be needing me."

Jordan chuckled and sat on the other side of Harrison's desk. They shared an office—they'd just started their PI business, and they didn't have much money to spend on rent yet, even with Jordan's second job as a liaison between the League and the city's police force—but Jordan was barely there usually, so it really was more Harrison's office.

"What do you have for me?" Harrison asked. Anything to get away from paperwork. He hadn't liked it when he was a detective, and he didn't like now that he was his own boss. Well, kind of. Jordan was his boss, really, but it felt more like they were partners, even though the business was technically Jordan's.

Jordan tapped his fingertips onto the desk. "I got a call from Jadon."

That made Harrison sit straighter in his chair. He might routinely work with demons now, even though they were wary of him and Jordan since they were humans, but the warriors fascinated him. The fact that Salomon, the demon he kind of had a crush on, was still staying at the League's HQ, didn't have anything to do with his interest.

Maybe.

Okay, it had a lot to do with it, but Harrison just wanted to do his job and help people and demons alike. The fact that he might get to ogle Sal in the process was just a nice bonus.

"What does he need?" Harrison asked.

"Sal finally managed to locate the demon who tried to kill Ilyhas and Esi. They're hiding in a human-only side of town, possibly working alongside humans. When he got the reading, the demon was in an office building, although Sal wasn't able to find out who it was. He was able to pinpoint the floor, though, and it's a law firm."

Harrison frowned. "Why would a demon work in a human law firm?"

"To hide? They have to know the League is looking for them, and they can't get to them where they are."

"But we can."

Jordan nodded. "We can. Well, you can in this case. I don't have the time to do this. The chief of police wants to see me about something or other."

"About demons?"

"No doubt. That's the only reason I have contacts with the police nowadays."

"So I'm in charge of this? I get to find the demon?"

"Yes. You're going to need to work with Sal and a few League warriors, no doubt. Jadon is expecting you tomorrow morning for a meeting. You'll get all the info. I took the liberty of checking the law firm up when he called me. There's a mailman job available. I know a few people there, and I managed to get you hired for the length of the investigation. They weren't happy about finding out that they have a demon in their midst."

Harrison had no trouble believing that. "So I'm a mail boy now?"

"As well as my partner, yeah. Jadon will tell you more, but don't put yourself in danger. Find the demon and report to him and whoever he puts in charge of this. They'll take it from there. They just need to be able to identify the demon."

"Got it. I could go now." It was getting late, but Harrison wasn't looking forward to going home to his empty apartment and eating dinner alone in front of the TV.

"Nah. Jadon thinks the demon is going to stay where they are since so far, they haven't been found. Take the night off, take care of whatever you need to take care of tomorrow so you don't have to come back here until the job is over, and go to HQ."

Damn. "Okay. You're going home to Caelan?"

Jordan's usual grim expression lightened, and he smiled the smile that was reserved to Caelan and any thoughts of him. "Yeah. He's off tonight, so we're going to take advantage of it."

"That's great. Have fun, then. I'll lock up, so go ahead and leave."

"You're sure?"

"Yeah." It wasn't like Harrison had anything better to do anyway.

He smiled when he heard Jordan whistle as he left the office. Jordan hadn't always been so happy. He still wasn't most of the time, but Caelan had a way of making him smile and softening him that Harrison hadn't thought he'd ever see. Jordan was different when he was with his boyfriend, as it should be. Harrison wanted what Jordan had with Caelan eventually, but so far, he hadn't had luck in that department.

Of course, if someone asked his dad, he'd say Harrison hadn't had luck in the job department either. He didn't like that Harrison wasn't a cop anymore, and he didn't waste a chance to tell Harrison how disappointed he was about that.

But Harrison didn't want to think about that right now. No, the only things he wanted to think about was his couch, a cold beer, a warm microwave meal, and a TV series—just not one about cops.

Harrison turned off his computer and left the office, making sure he locked the door. He dragged his ass home after briefly wondering if he should go to a bar. Underworld, maybe? He was human, but they were as welcome as humans at Underworld, even though the place was owned by a half-demon. Harrison wasn't sure he was up for the noise, though, and he certainly wasn't for the vigilance he'd need to hang out at Underworld. He might be friends with the owner, and humans might be welcome there, but that didn't mean no one was going to try to start something with him. Demons tended to be confrontational even on their best days, and they weren't usually happy to find a human encroaching on what they viewed as their territory.

Home it was, then.

Harrison trudged to his apartment. He had to take the bus, which he hated, but it was near to impossible to find a parking spot at the office, and the few there were reserved for clients.

The bus stank, though, and it was slow going. When Harrison finally got off, the only thing he wanted to do was take a shower and bury in bed, so of course, he found Icha waiting for the elevator.

Harrison almost groaned. He liked the oni demon, but Icha always tried to get into Harrison's pants, and Harrison wasn't sure he had the energy to fend him off tonight. It looked like he was going to have to try, though, because Icha had noticed him.

"Harry!" he crowed.

Harrison glared. "My name's Harrison, not Harry. You know that."

Icha touched Harrison's arm. "I know, but Harry rolls off

the tongue better, don't you think? I could demonstrate it to you. It would be perfect for screaming while you're fucking me."

Harrison didn't like the fact that he blushed every time Icha tried anything with him—which was every time their paths crossed. They lived on the same floor, and Icha frequently came around to borrow sugar or whatnot, usually wearing little to nothing. Harrison was perpetually blushing in his presence, and Icha seemed to find it hilarious and possibly arousing. Harrison couldn't stop it, so he tried to avoid Icha as much as he could.

He didn't always succeed.

Icha ran his hand up Harrison's arm. "You know it would be good."

Harrison barked out a laugh. "I don't doubt that."

"Then why don't you give in?"

Harrison had been tempted more times than he remembered. He could give in and have sex with Icha. It would be fun and light-hearted because that was how Icha was. And it would be good.

But Harrison wasn't a one-night stand kind of guy, and that was all Icha was offering. Even if he wanted more, Harrison doubted that would work between them. He didn't like Icha that way, the way he liked Sal, no matter how ridiculous that sounded. There was no changing it, though.

Harrison was relieved when the elevator doors opened. He was going to have to ride up with Icha, but he knew how to keep the demon at bay by now.

Icha squeezed Harrison's ass only twice before the elevator stopped at their floor and Harrison rushed out. Icha followed him at a more sedate pace, pouting. "When are you going to make me happy?" he asked.

"When are you going to be ready for a relationship?"

Icha grimaced. "Never, I hope. It's just not me."

"And fucking around is just not me."

Icha grinned. "Maybe, but I sure as hell am having fun

trying to convince you it is."

ABOUT THE AUTHOR

Catherine lives in Italy, country of good food and hot men. She used to write fantasy as a child, but it was reading her first gay erotic romance novel that made her realize that that was what she really wanted to write.

After graduating from college in English language and translation, she divides her day between writing, reading, taking care of her son and reading some more.

You can find her on Facebook and Twitter or on her website: authorcatherinelievens.wordpress.com

Email: lievens.catherine@gmail.com

Newsletter: http://eepurl.com/c-uvKn